Afghan
Silk

I0554447

Afghan Silk

JULIA SCOTT

TIGER OF THE STRIPE

First published in 2008 by
TIGER OF THE STRIPE
50 Albert Road
Richmond
Surrey TW10 6DP
United Kingdom

ALL CHARACTERS IN THIS WORK ARE FICTITIOUS
AND NO RESEMBLANCE TO
ANY REAL PERSON IS INTENDED.

ISBN 978-1-940799-33-7

CHAPTER I

THE CRACK OF GUNFIRE took Michael by surprise. There was no way to escape the bullets. A major in the Fifth Gurkha Rifles, he had been on many campaigns, but this attack was different. He did not hear any bullet whistle past; he only heard the echo of the explosion from the slopes of the arid hills. It was loud, and he felt confused. Time seemed to slow up. Instinctively he took shelter behind an outcrop of rocks, yet every movement took a strange amount of effort. His body seemed extraordinarily heavy and he felt breathless, labouring to fill his lungs with air. While he heard his brigade return fire from behind him, he distractedly put his hand on his shirt where he felt a dull pain. It felt sticky. He looked at his fingers and gasped. They were red with blood. He looked down to see a dark stain spreading quickly, and he felt a rising panic as he strained for breath. He was dizzy.

'If it was bad, the pain would be worse,' he told himself.

The intense brightness of the Afghan sun grew dark.

'Home!' he thought. 'I've let them down. I can't die. Not now. Not here. Not after this summer.'

His knees crumpled under him, and his day turned to night, as he lost consciousness.

Camberley, England. Three months earlier

'You're going to die, Michael.'

Gladys Rogers sat on the edge of her plush Victorian sofa, her grey hair neatly crimped, her silk blouse expertly ironed. Her son was startled and put his newspaper down to look at her. She was normally so practical and busy, with little time for serious reflection. But now there was pain in her eyes. He had not seen her so preoccupied since his father had died, four years ago. She placed her hands in her lap, one on top of the other, as if to force herself into a calm pose.

Gladys was a true product of this quiet, suburban and very English town. It did not have the history of other settlements of its size. There were no roman walls, no medieval monuments, and only ersatz Tudor houses, built by stockbroker types and red-brick Edwardian villas, like Gladys's genteel residence. But what Camberley lacked in ancient splendor, it made up for in what the locals liked to think of as quiet decency. Many of its inhabitants would have borrowed a term current in the British Raj. Camberley was a 'pukka' sort of place. It had class. Locals used a lot of those Indian words, not only because they thought it gave them an air of authority as veterans of the Empire, but because many of them had actually served in India all their working lives, as army officers. Camberley was a magnet for military families due to its most famous landmark – the large military college, Sandhurst. The town actually owed its existence to the College, and had been founded in the early 1800s to house its officers. On the poorer side of town, humble dwellings were built for their servants and tradesmen, a convenient segregation.

Gladys, like her home town, was not of ancient lineage, but she was, without question, a gentlewoman. After all, she kept a large house, with three servants, and a gardener. Her husband had not been an army officer, but had held a responsible position in a prestigious London bank, where he had commuted by train each day. Nobody in Camberley was likely to peer too closely into Gladys's pedigree, as the snobbish families of the old cathedral towns would have done, and that suited her very well. Not that she was ashamed of her forbears. She was far too proud to be intimidated by that sort of nonsense. She was simply content to be judged by her current respectable home and her own impeccable appearance. Now, as she addressed her son, she tried to maintain a calm, dignified manner, but, given the subject she was raising with him, it would be difficult to keep an unruffled pose.

'If you don't take action now, you'll be killed. So many have died,' she continued. 'John Fairbrother, that new young subaltern, the colonel's son.' 'I don't want you to go back. You're my only child.' She paused. 'And then you have to think about Sarah.'

Sarah was Michael's fiancée and the daughter of a retired colonel.

'She'll be here within the hour and I want you to pay her more attention. You've been ignoring her lately, and I don't know why.'

Michael frowned. He did not want his mother interfering with his romantic life. He knew she approved of Sarah, who was from a 'suitable' background and a neighbour. That should have been enough to satisfy her. It also irritated him that she was giving him advice as her child. He was a battle-seasoned officer, and looked the part. The word 'child' was not one that fitted him. He had stopped being a child since he was unceremoniously sent off to boarding school at the age of seven.

He was taller than most of his fellow officers. The armchair he was sitting in was too small for him and his knees stuck up in an ungainly way. Yet he had elegance about him. His thick dark hair was combed back from his forehead with pomade and he had classical features. His nose was straight and his cheekbones high. The only childish thing about him was his clothes. They looked rumpled, like an active schoolboy's.

'I want you to fix the wedding date,' Gladys continued. 'You couldn't find a better girl than Sarah, although I know she has her critics. People don't understand that she's a no-nonsense sort of girl. They think she's tactless. Sarah wouldn't hesitate to tell you what your priorities were. She would keep you out of danger and help you settle down. Don't you think?'

Michael ignored the question about Sarah. It made him uncomfortable and he did not know why. He wanted to reassure his mother about his safety but he had his own sense of foreboding. He had seen many deaths lately. John Fairbrother, his friend and neighbour from childhood, had been killed in front of him. He was still wrestling with the horror of it. Hostilities were increasing. He recently had a premonition of his own death in a dream. He was being carried on a stretcher over bumpy ground. Everything around him faded away till he could not see and then the dream abruptly ended. Nightmares of combat and hideous injuries had started to intrude on his sleep, and even Gladys had noticed a change in his behavior. They had been in town recently and had just come out of the teashop when a stupid thing happened. A car backfired, and Michael started violently. Afterwards he could not hide the fact that he was shaking, and his mother looked at him anxiously. It would have been better if she had made a comment, but she just scrutinized him silently. He was now determined to act carefree, for her sake.

It was July of 1934, and Michael was at home on leave from his regiment in India. It was an elite body of men. Michael was with the Gurkhas, a legendary force that defended the northwest frontier of India. The regiment took its name from the soldiers it recruited from Nepal. The Gurkha men were stationed with the British in their hillside garrisons in the foothills of the Himalayas, and, like the British, some had family with them. They went on campaign with the British in the anarchic hills of India and Afghanistan, trying to subdue the belligerent tribesmen, the Pathan. These guerilla warriors ruled by terror. Devout Muslims encouraged by their religious scholars, they wanted no infidel to dictate their actions. They wanted to be free to settle feuds between themselves with blood shed, to raid peaceful villages in Indian territory, and to fire upon anyone they saw as an intruder.

Michael's hatred of the Pathan had been cemented by one horrific episode. Before this one event, he had no illusions about the potential ruthlessness of his own side. They left doctored clips of ammunition for the tribesmen, always short of ammunition, to pick up. When the Pathan tried to fire the bullets they would blow up catastrophically in their hands and faces. His regiment rarely took prisoners, especially if there was no civilian government employee in the area to check up on them. Similar brutalities were expected from the enemy. But nothing could surpass the horror of that one day that he would never forget. A British officer had been badly injured and the battalion had tried to rescue him twice. They had to give up when their losses became too great. Then Michael was the first to find the man's body. He had been flayed, possibly while still alive, and his skin was pegged out, with his genitals excised.

The British had two choices. They could try to quash the border tribes, but this would be impossible. The vast terrain was mountainous and could not be monitored. The tribes were disparate and no treaty would be kept by them all. The other option was to adopt a 'live and let live' arrangement. The British would keep the frontier intact and appease the tribes with gifts, negotiations and, when this did not work, the threat of force. This carrot and stick approach succeeded much of the time, but the tribes chafed under the domination of the 'infidels'. Every so often they would attack British soldiers or wage an all-out rebellion. There would be fighting, and then it would subside as quickly as it started. There would be an uneasy peace for a time, with only the occasional sniper fire from a disgruntled tribesman or a young Pathan trying to prove his warrior status.

And now Michael was in another world; suburban England, where only the dignity and propriety of army life was allowed to surface. Death in battle was seen as clean and heroic, even if the prospect did deprive mothers, like Gladys, of their sleep. Michael did not want his mother to raise the issue now. He was taking his leave to sort out his wedding plans and to take a rest from combat, after a long stint of dealing with bloody uprisings in the Northwest Frontier and Bengal. He had desperately wanted to forget, for a while at least, the ugliness of military violence. But the languorous boat trip home, with the fancy dress parties, the formal dinners, and the hours of relaxing on deck in the sun had not settled him. Neither had the familiar surroundings of home. In fact his return had made matters worse. He felt at odds with all those around him, who had no idea of what he had experienced in India. He felt jumpy and isolated. And now his mother was reminding him of battle. Even Sarah was no comfort to him. It was as if there was a part of him that would always be a stranger to her. Yet he felt sure he could resolve their differences. Sarah would fit in as an army wife, even if he had to stay in India and she was forced to live in the confines of the regiment's hill station. She would adapt and he could see her as a leading light among the handful of officer's wives, who spent their time visiting each other in their sparse but comfortable bungalows, organizing the servants, and dining in the club house. She would be in her element, thought Michael, gossiping about a haughty colonel's wife and laughing at some faux pas a junior officer had made. Sarah would also enjoy the prestige of the regiment.

'I take good care of myself, mum. Things have been heating up lately, but they'll be quieter soon,' said Michael.

'Heating up! Is that what you call it? The British are being led by the nose. That half naked fakir … what's his name?'

'Gandhi, mum. And he happens to be a respected lawyer. Trained in London at Middle Temple. Can't get more 'Establishment' than that! '

'Well, why doesn't he dress like a lawyer?' said Gladys. 'He even came to England in that indecent loin cloth.'

'Mum, please talk sensibly,' said Michael. He wondered when Sarah would arrive to distract his mother from her worries. He felt the strain of attempting to look impassive and of keeping her off the scent of his secrets, and he had many. The secret of the rage he felt inside, ever since John Fairbrother's death that was obsessing him night and day, that he knew would only be abated by hate-filled combat. The secret that he had recently drafted his will and a farewell letter, in case anything should happen to him. The secret of what he had promised to do for John in India. His mother knew an engagement was like a legal contract, so she should relax, he thought, and give Sarah and himself some more time. He decided to exaggerate his air of insouciance and to be funny.

'It's all your fault, mother! Remember those comic books, *Chums,* you bought for me as a child? They were all about the derring-do of British soldiers and the romance of the Northwest Frontier. No blood and guts. Just fighting noble savages needing to learn the British way. They made me long to be a Beau Geste. You should have given me Robin Hood stories. Then I would have stayed at home and been a tax man – robbing the rich to pay the poor.'

Gladys looked prim. 'It's always a mother's fault, isn't it?' she said. 'And I've always told you, sarcasm is unbecoming. You're using it far too frequently.' She looked him in the eye, as if to penetrate his thoughts. 'You've changed, Michael, and it worries me. There's a hardness about you I've never seen before. It's the trauma of seeing that officer's body after he was mutilated by the Pathan, isn't it? Has fighting those barbarians turned your senses? I'm beginning to think so.'

'I can't say I like the Pathan,' said Michael, conscious of his understatement. He had often felt alone in his loathing for the Pathan while some of his fellow officers had expressed admiration for their courage and single-mindedness. He tried to justify his antipathy. 'I'm not alone. John Nicholson, that Indian Mutiny hero, called them the most bloodthirsty race in existence. You know what else he said? That they would sell their own relations if the price was right. And they would! They would sell their little old granny to the highest bidder.'

Gladys spoke gently, her lips pursed. She then spoke gently, as if she were the family doctor, wearily explaining the lack of cure for the common cold. 'Let's face it, dear, British India is finished and you're fighting a lost cause.'

Michael reacted so violently to her words, Gladys grabbed her pearl necklace in shock and seemed to be in danger of breaking the thread and scattering the precious roundels all over the Persian rug. She watched her son's face become flushed as his voice grew louder

'It's not a lost cause. Can't you see? Support me, at least! John didn't die for nothing. We've given India railways, a legal system, science, education. I like India and believe in what we're doing and that's why I'm a soldier. And I can't say I'm a saint.' He suddenly spoke quietly, almost mumbling to himself. 'In fact I nearly killed a prisoner the other day.'

Michael regretted his confession as soon as he had made it and seen his mother's reaction. He tried to soften the revelation. 'Don't look at me like that, mum! You don't need to be horrified. I didn't kill him, although I was very tempted to do so. Your moral judgment, all those finer feelings you helped to teach me, tend to white out in battle.'

He wanted to change the subject, but Gladys was looking at him silently, waiting for an explanation. It seemed a sacrilege that the distant and bloody world of the Northwest Frontier would have to make an appearance, through his own words, in this tranquil English sitting room, with its gently ticking clocks, and Victorian grandparents smiling benignly from their painted portraits. He outlined the facts as baldly as he could to avoid upsetting his mother.

It had happened so quickly. A young sergeant, fresh from England, had been killed by a sniper. Soon afterwards an officer with an uncanny second sense arrested what appeared to be a veiled woman, with large dirty feet in battered leather sandals that stuck out under her black robe. Everyone thought the officer was mad to pick on such a poor-looking peasant. But when her veil was torn off, the 'woman' was revealed as a man. There was another surprise. Under the robes was a gun that had recently been discharged. It was, in all probability, the same gun that had killed the young sergeant. Michael had felt an intense rage. The urge to shoot the assassin was overwhelming. The man had hidden himself so cunningly, and had picked on the sergeant who had no chance to defend himself. It seemed unjust that soldiers had been forced to learn restraint when they dealt with such crazed killers. But vengeance of the Gurkhas was more subtle than Michael's unspoken plans. They had taken the gun out of sight and bent the barrel very slightly. They gave it back to the tribesman, knowing that when he next pulled the trigger, it would explode, catastrophically for the man.

Gladys was exasperated after listening to the story. Her usual calm, patrician manners were falling apart and her eyes were welling with tears. Then she suddenly started to cry. She tried to stifle her emotion, shielding her eyes with her hand, but her shoulders shook uncontrollably and her breathing was racked with sobs. It was painful for Michael to watch his mother's anguish. She did not normally show her emotion. She was usually too busy, controlled and controlling. Michael wanted to reach out to her and to reassure her but he was too discomfited. Her outburst produced feelings in him that he did not want to examine. He had to talk to spare himself the embarrassment of her weeping. But no words came.

Gladys dabbed her eyes with a silk handkerchief she pulled out of the sleeve of her blouse. 'You're telling me about these horrors and yet you insist on returning.'

'I can't understand it,' Michael said. 'You're the one who encouraged me to join the army. You are always the one to wave the flag and say "my country, right or wrong". What's happened to you mum?' His mother's doubts unsettled him. He knew inwardly that there was a darker motivation than patriotism pushing him to return to fighting. Although Michael felt patriotic, his most recent war experiences were forcing the same questions into his mind that his mother was voicing.

Gladys shot her son a fierce glance. 'No one could call me unpatriotic. No one! But I'm a mother and I have common sense. Michael, there are other ways you could serve your country. I keep thinking about the tragic death of John Fairbrother. Where did his service to India get him?' Gladys's voice became dangerously tremulous. 'A place in some far-flung, neglected cemetery. Have you seen his parents? They're broken. Listen to me, Michael…'

Gladys was interrupted by the high-pitched door bell. The housemaid, a young girl called Doris, who was so small she looked like a child dressing up when she wore her black and white uniform, called to them from the hallway.

'I've got it Mrs Rogers, ma'am.'

They listened in silence to the sound of a woman's heels clacking over the floorboards, and then muffled by the rug outside. The door opened brusquely. It was Sarah, Michael's fiancée. She walked without hesitation into the room. Michael was pleased to see her. He found her attractive, even though she was a little plump, and had little fashion sense. The strange thing was that she thought she was modish, but somehow her efforts fell flat. The dresses were always a little too tight, the colors a little too bright, the tailoring lumpy. She carried a handbag as if she were about to swing it into someone's groin. But Michael liked her spirit. It was irrepressible. Some people called her bossy, insensitive, but Michael thought her forthright. She had been his first girlfriend, the typical girl-next-door. Their relationship had drifted imperceptibly from friendship into romantic attachment, partly because they had been together so often before Michael went to India, and partly because a liaison is what both sets of parents expected of them. Michael could now rely on Sarah to lighten the conversation.

'I'm not intruding, am I?' The question was rhetorical. Gladys tucked her handkerchief back inside her sleeve and blinked away the dampness in her eyes, forcing herself to smile a little too obviously. Sarah sat down heavily in an armchair and sighed as if her abrupt way of doing every-thing, from walking, to speaking had, for once, tired her. She looked at them for the first time. 'You both look a bit glum. Well, as they say, cheer up, it may never happen. By the way, that's what daddy is trying to tell everyone now. People keep going on and on about the Germans and how they're frightened there will be another war. They're so te-dious. Daddy says its absolute nonsense. He says if only we had a public works program like the Germans we might get this country back on its feet again. If only there were more people like daddy.'

Sarah's father was Colonel Traverse, a retired army officer who was constantly forming committees to reform society's inadequacies. There had been a Committee for a Union-free Town that had come to nothing when they were locked out of meeting rooms by unionized town jani-tors; there had been a Citizens for Decency Committee, to improve the dress code in town shops and restaurants. That had also foundered when the daughter of a local luminary had complained to her father of harass-ment when she had gone to the ice cream parlor in a skimpy halter-neck creation. Then there had been the English Patriots' League. It was the brainchild of the colonel and was a loose association of rightwing sym-pathizers, advocating tighter links with Germany and spouting anti-Bolshevik rhetoric. The colonel had even put a brass plaque outside the private small office he kept in town to advertise its existence. The local police commissioner had to advise the colonel that it was not quite 'the thing' for Camberley when some out-of-town thugs had created a distur-bance at the office door, throwing beer bottles and chanting words that had never polluted the delicate airs of Camberley before that day.

Gladys smiled at Sarah.

'I was just telling Michael I thought it unwise to return to India.'

'I wouldn't worry about that, Mrs Rogers! Michael and I have discussed it. I'm perfectly happy to go to India when we marry. Don't worry about me. Remember that friend of mine, Bella?'

Michael interrupted. 'Why is it that you always have friends with extraordinary names, Sarah? Bella, Debs.'

'I don't think they're extraordinary. But as I was saying, Bella is having a ball out in India.'

Michael laughed. 'The Bella of the ball!' he said. Sarah frowned.

'Mrs Rogers, I know you worry about me, and it's so sweet. But there's no problem. I'll be fine.'

Suddenly Sarah started laughing. Gladys and Michael looked at her, perplexed.

'It's funny. It's just too funny.'

Gladys sounded irritated for the first time.

'What is funny, dear?'

'A friend of mine said that I would have problems when I married Michael. She said that men at the hill station far outnumbered the women, and that an attractive girl like me would be a terrible distraction, even though I would be married.'

'I don't think there's any danger of that,' said Michael. Sarah's face fell.

'Oh', she said, and Michael saw that he had offended her.

'What I mean is that there is a very strong sense of honour in the army and a married woman can feel perfectly safe from embarrassment.'

Sarah smiled. 'Yes. That's right. Anyway, I've got bags of time to prepare. I'm going to be a busy bee with all the wedding preparations. I just wish Michael would do more. We've only got about 18 months. Did you know we plan to go shopping for the ring soon, Mrs Rogers?'

'No, I hadn't heard,' said Gladys.

'Michael, you never tell your mother anything. And then there's the photo I have to have taken for the announcement in the Tatler. Did you see Vera's announcement portrait. Poor Vera. The hair was an absolute mess. She should have listened to me. I told her where to go. '

'You always know where to tell people to go,' said Michael. The temptation to tease Sarah was irresistible, he did not know why. She looked back at him, but Michael gave no hint of whether he was being ironic.

'Vera's such a charming girl' said Mrs Rogers.

'Yes, she is,' said Sarah. 'You would never guess her grandfather was a baker from the East End of London.'

Michael saw his mother squirm in her chair, and he remembered her own background. Sarah continued.

'But she really is very pleasant. She can be a little opinionated, sometimes, just a teensy bit stubborn. Like with the hair for the photo. She doesn't know when to take advice.'

Gladys turned to her son. 'Where are you going to shop for the ring?' she asked him.

Michael felt cornered.

Sarah answered before Michael could draw breath.

'Mappin and Webb. It's where the royals shop. I'd really like to have it ready in time for the Garden Party.'

Gladys gasped. 'My garden party! I still have so much to do. It seems like the whole town is coming. Are your parents coming, Sarah?' Michael saw that his mother had more and more diva-like mannerisms. She was more active these days in the Amateur Dramatics Society and Michael was not sure if it was good for her.

'Rather! Mum has even bought a new hat. It'll be just like the King's Garden Party. By the way, did you know that daddy thinks he might be invited to the Palace Garden Party? His work for that charity for genteel older folk was noticed, apparently. What do they call those people? 'Distressed Gentle Folk'. Dad calls them 'Distressing gentle folk'. He says he could nominate quite a few neighbours for that title. Between you and me, he doesn't have much patience with the elderly.' Without stopping for breath she asked abruptly, 'Is there any tea on offer?'

Gladys smiled. 'How remiss of me! Of course! It's waiting for us so I'll just ring for it to be brought in.' She got up to press the bell by the fireplace.

The door opened so suddenly it gave Sarah a start. There was a great noise of rattling and muttering as Mrs Waller, the plump middle-aged housekeeper, still in her cooking apron, maneuvered a heavily laden tea trolley slowly into the room. Michael realised her usual curiosity had led her to bring in the tea, a job that she would normally have delegated to young Doris. He felt he could see her straining to listen to any conversation. She gave Sarah a look of outright hostility that Sarah failed to notice. Michael realised she must have heard Sarah's comments about the elderly from outside the door, because Mrs Waller cared devotedly for an aged mother. He knew, in any case, that she did not like Sarah, and was always looking for ammunition against her. He had caught her talking about her in the kitchen with his aunt one day who only made half-hearted attempts to stop her gossip. Mrs Waller made sure that nothing escaped her notice in the house.

'Dear girl!' said Gladys. Michael thought once more that his mother's florid outpourings were becoming a problem. It was strange how Sarah seemed to bring out this behaviour in her. 'Your father's going to have to put up with quite a few of our older pensioners at the party. But don't you worry. There are plenty of young ones. There is that new neighbour, Mrs Weinstein's granddaughter. She has had to leave Germany because...' Gladys paused and leaned forward to make a dramatic hissing whisper, '...she's Jewish.'

'Oh, I knew that, Mrs Rogers,' said Sarah. 'Ruth! She's caused quite a stir already.'

Michael was getting impatient with his mother and with Sarah. 'It's very easy to cause a stir in Camberley,' he said. 'All you have to do is get your dog to cock his leg at the wrong lamp post.'

'Michael, you're being puerile,' said his mother, as she poured the tea and looked irked.

Sarah looked to the ceiling in exasperation before speaking. 'As I was saying, she is getting the reputation of being a little showy. I saw her in town the other day and it looked as if she were dressed up for the Ritz.'

'Her grandmother was a beautiful woman in her day," said Gladys

'Ruth's a little dark' said Sarah. 'But who am I to say?'

'Very humble of you, Sarah' said Michael. Sarah looked at Michael, suspicious of his tone.

'We'll have to judge for ourselves,' he added.

'If only it were good judgement', said Gladys. 'You young people, you can't think properly for yourselves. You think you are immortal. At my age you see how fragile life is.'

Sarah was not listening and was busy trying to salvage some cake she had dropped on the carpet. Michael saw her suck the icing off her fingers, and he grimaced involuntarily at her action.

Gladys continued, looking only at Michael.

'I don't know', she said. 'I have a feeling Michael has something to hide from us. This determination to return to India at all costs. After John Fairbrother's death, too. I don't understand it.'

Michael looked at his mother. He had always credited her with a second sense. He suspected that she knew he had doubts about sacrificing all 'for king and country'. He suspected also that she knew he did indeed have a hidden motive to return to India. But that was absurd, he thought. Not even Gladys was clairvoyant, and as for her warning that he could die, it was unfair of her to talk like that. Stupid. Yet he couldn't ignore her words. They kept echoing in his ears. 'You're going to die, Michael.'

MICHAEL COULD NOT FIND Sarah at the garden party. He wondered why she was avoiding him. He sensed that he had been too reticent with her lately and that he would have to make up for it. Suddenly, as he looked at the crowd, he saw a stranger at the edge of the garden by the fence. She looked out of place, and isolated. No one was talking to her. Her silk floral dress was a little too elegant for Camberley. Her hair was too dark and straight to be English, and her nose, though it suited her face and gave her a distinguished look, was unusually prominent. She could be French, he thought, or partly Asian. He was reminded of a beautiful woman back in India, an Anglo-Indian, whom he knew he would be seeing on his return. The thought disconcerted him and so he focused on the stranger with renewed concentration, but then he reminded himself that he had to find Sarah. She would expect him to look for her first. She would be waiting for him to approach her and to pay her court.

He looked over the top of the crowd, making himself still taller on tiptoe. He saw such contrasts in the people before him that he felt like an anthropologist studying strange tribal habits. Everyone was wearing hats and many of the women's hats were flamboyant and decked with flowers while the men wore straw panamas. But the headgear of humbler guests was glaringly different from the rest of the group. It gave them a battered look and many of the poorer women still wore the cloche style of the 20's. The working men, if they wore any hats, wore the flat tweed caps of their class. It would have seemed 'uppity' to wear anything else.

Looking at the poorer crowd, he knew that he would not find Sarah there. She prided herself on the way she managed servants and tradesmen. She had said to Michael, 'People who get too friendly with servants land themselves in trouble. It's not kindness, it just confuses them. No! You have to be firm and authoritative.'

But Michael had felt ill-at-ease listening to her. And now, as he looked at the people from the 'wrong' side of town he was reminded of the effects of the Depression. People were still having problems finding work and could not afford new clothes. Sometimes they could not even afford to go to the doctor. The poor were hit far worse than the upper classes. As he stood in the middle of the party Michael remembered the last time he had been on leave in England. India had not prepared him for what he found in his own country where he had been raised so comfortably. In India he had seen it all. An old man dying in the arms of a wizened old lady. A woman who had just had her baby in a makeshift shelter of cardboard. But to see shoeless children in the London streets and women begging in darkened doorways, trying to hide their shame, was deeply shocking to him. The sight of them gave him a strange empty feeling deep inside and he wished there was a way to help them.

He looked at his affluent neighbours who, even now, were probably grumbling about the money and work that they had lost after the Stock Market crash. They were oblivious of the struggles of the other towns-people who were standing at their elbow. Michael had always accepted class differences as being a manifestation of the diversity of English society. But he was beginning to suspect that class distinctions, like military imperatives, mostly served the upper levels of the establishment.

'Where is Sarah?' He felt impatient to find her and elbowed his way forward. As he looked, his gaze unconsciously drifted towards the elegant woman, still standing in the same place, and now talking to a middle-aged woman.

His thoughts were interrupted by someone speaking in his ear. It was his mother and he realized that he had been staring a little too intently at the young woman.

'That's Ruth, Mrs Weinstein's grand daughter. Remember Mrs Weinstein? She was always out walking those two dachshunds. As I told you, Ruth has come from Germany and has had a very rough time of it there.'

Gladys paused and looked at her son.

'Don't get any ideas, Michael. She also has a young son, and no one knows who or where the father is.'

As Gladys was speaking, her sister appeared at her side. She was his mother's twin, but she looked very different. Instead of Gladys's trim, conservative looks. Estelle was small and tubby. Still, thought Michael, she looks elegant with her fashionably tailored dress, her crimped hair, and that outlandish, feathered hat posed at such a coquettish angle.

Gladys spoke quickly, as if to shut out any opposition. 'Your aunt and I have both noticed the same thing. You're not paying enough attention to Sarah.'

'I can't even find her mum!' said Michael.

Don't be ridiculous! What sort of excuse is that? We have a nice, large garden. Michael, but it's hardly Windsor Great Park!'

Estelle spoke up in her usual sweet-toned voice, but Michael heard a trace of irony in her words. 'Sarah isn't the sort of girl to be easily camouflaged, is she? Any way, she can find Michael if she wants to and I haven't just come to talk to Michael about Sarah.'

Gladys continued, ignoring her sister, who was failing to show a united front

'Sarah is here somewhere and she looks very put out. I've said my piece now. I'm trying to run this whole operation. Trying to keep every-one happy. By the way, Estelle, that hat looks extremely silly. It doesn't suit you at all.' Without waiting for a reaction from her sister, Gladys took up the pose of a choreographer.

'Edith, take those finger sandwiches over there, and Edward,' she caught the elbow of a serious young man with a tray of tea cups, 'You're needed in that corner.'

Michael could not muster the same enthusiasm that he saw all around him, especially since he had seen the attractive young neighbour. He felt nervous, ambivalent. The presence of all those familiar faces should feel so comforting, he thought, but he was starting to see class differences as imposed, divisive and alienating one group from another He expected an atmosphere of bonhomie, but instead he felt a strange sadness and loneliness, that reminded him of being at boarding school, as he stood under the unfamiliar, gentle English sun. The anger that had kept nagging him since the start of his leave, returned to him now. He had an insane desire to approach the pompous local bank manager, Bovis, who was standing nearby in beige suit that was more Co-Op than Saville Row. He wanted to say 'Don't let me disturb you, but I just wanted to tell you what combat is really like. The uncensored version. Forget the uniforms. They're elegant all right, but war is ugly. A stenching slaughter house. You're the sort of chap who loves uniforms. But don't let me interrupt your tea.'

Then there were the veterans. It was only sixteen years since the end of the Great War, and many of the older men present witnessed terrible things that no one should ever have to endure. It was all hidden away, now. 'Plastered over like a harlot's face,' thought Michael, remembering a line from his schoolboy Shakespeare. Amiability and good humor were the order of the day and the strongest thing was supposed to be the tea. He, too, was expected to play the game, to satisfy everyone's preconceptions. His role, he knew, was to be the returned son, paired up with one of their own kind, happy to do his part in India for the Empire, happy to be welcomed back into the community.

Michael sighed, and turned his attention to more pleasant things. He had been enjoying looking at Ruth when his mother had interrupted him. To avoid further interference from his mother, he would have to delay before approaching her. He would also put off finding Sarah, especially if she was with her father. Instead, he would do his duty and approach Ron Bovis, the bank manager. He saw Ruth look over at him in what he thought was curiosity. It made him all the more keen to play the role of suave host.

There was another reason for greeting Mr Bovis. Michael knew he was feeling sore. He had just been the star of the local amateur dramatics society. Gladys had directed him in Julius Caesar and it had been a disaster. Michael had seen it the evening after his arrival and had winced in embarrassment at the final scene. After spluttering out, 'Et tu Brute?' he had groaned and staggered around the stage like a skewered bull. By the time he came to his death line, 'Then fall Caesar,' his voice was drowned out in cat calls and laughter from the more uncouth elements in the audience. There were shouts of 'Get him off!'

Michael decided on a conciliatory approach.

'Mr Bovis. How good to see you again. I must come to see you for some financial advice. You're the only person I trust outside the City.'

Bovis looked haughty rather than gratified. His nostrils flared slightly. He had a strange way of speaking, spluttering his words as if he could not get them out fast enough, and pronouncing his *r*s as *w*s. 'You'd better make an appointment. I find myself vewy busy, since my last pwomotion.'

Michael wanted to complete the sentence for him, 'fielding theatre scouts falling over themselves to sign you up', but he just smiled. He shot a glance at Ruth and was pleased to see her looking at him. She quickly avoided his gaze.

Bovis also smiled. But it was a strange, unctuous smile that reeked of hypocricy and it was not directed at Michael. One of Bovis' wealthy clients, Mrs Stanthorp, was edging past with difficulty because of her bulk. She was carrying a plate piled perilously high with cake and sandwiches. In her fifties, Mrs Stanthorp was tall as well as stout, and was known by a cruel but apt nickname in the neighbourhood – 'Mrs High and Mighty'.

'Looks like it might wain, Mrs Stanthorp,' said Bovis.

Mrs Stanthorp glanced up at a menacing dark cloud, and then at Bovis, with a glint in her eye.

'Hail, Caesar!'

She roared in laughter at her own joke, and Bovis could only smile pathetically and look into his empty tea cup. In spite of his pompousness, Michael felt sorry for him. Bovis suddenly seemed an outsider like him. An unlikely fellow-traveller, but a comrade nonetheless. Once Mrs Stanthorp was well out of earshot, Bovis expressed his anger to Michael.

'I'm out of place in this town. Just because some of us are more cultured, we have to be a target. I'm sure your mother feels the same. Even that Colonel Twaverse had to have a go. I never expected it fwom him. Walked into the pub one lunch time and yelled out "Whiskey and toga, Bovis?" It's ignowance. Sheer ignowance.'

'Quite, quite,' said Michael, trying to suppress his laughter. His mood had suddenly lifted. He looked over at Ruth. She was now talking to a young woman holding a baby. Her figure was perfect, thought Michael. Her slim-line dress, cinched at the waist, showed off her height and proportions. He imagined putting his arm around the slim waist, of drawing her near to him. He approached as casually as he could. He felt nervous, in spite of the fact that he normally felt at ease with women. He had even managed some quite successful flirtations on leave at hill stations in India, though, except for one lapse, he was too upright to carry them further, and of course there was his attachment to Sarah to consider.

He had trouble finding an opening topic of conversation with Ruth after the introductions were made. 'It's good to meet you at last', she said after the pause. She smiled pleasantly and held out her hand. There was just a hint of a German accent in her voice. He could not speak as he grasped her hand, trying to focus on the formality of the gesture. Her grasp was gentle and warm, and he realized with embarrassment that he held on to her just a fraction too long. The woman with the baby sensed the tension and left them alone, which made the situation worse. Their silence was eloquent, and they smiled at each other, in some sort of unspoken acknowledgement. Their eyes met and they quickly looked down in embarrassment. As he stood beside her, Michael noticed her long, slim, bronzed arms. He would now have to make polite conversation, and the arms were so distracting.

Michael was now fixed by her dark eyes and when Ruth saw his confusion, she tried to dispel it.

'I've just moved into my grandmother's house. I spent quite a lot of time there when I was a child.'

'That's why your English is almost perfect.'

'It's kind of you to say so.'

'Other than that, you've lived in Germany, I hear.' Michael was irritated that he stumbled over his words like a shy adolescent.

'Yes.' Ruth frowned slightly, as if she did not want to talk more of it. 'Have you been here long?'

'Since I was a boy. Well, I was mostly at boarding school, so I was really only here in the holidays. I vaguely know your grandmother'. He was talking without thinking what he was saying. He felt there was a silent conversation between them. He had never known how pleasant it could be to feel nervous.

There was another awkward silence. Michael already knew he wanted to see her again, he was sure it would not offend Sarah. Ruth was a neighbour, who knew nobody. It was only courteous to befriend her. Any minute he would have to go and make conversation with other people. How could he ask her without being abrupt? If he did not act quickly he would lose his chance.

'Do you play tennis?'

'Yes, I love to play.'

'Well, we have a court. Not a very good one. It's grass and there are too may lumps and bumps. But it works. It's just over there.' He pointed towards a line of hedges.

It was just then that he spotted Sarah advancing on him. She had obviously tired of waiting for him to find her. She was in a loud floral dress, just a bit too short and too tight. She looked like a plump, hearty farmer's wife. Her brown curled hair bounced as she walked. She waved in an exaggerated way, as if she thought Michael would overlook her. An impossibility. No one could overlook Sarah, he thought.

Michael waved back in greeting, but he felt unexpectedly sheepish. Sarah, after all, was so pleasant and such good fun. She would make a good wife, he thought.

Sarah was shouting to be heard from a distance.

'Michael, there you are. I can't believe how many people there are here.'

Though he would have preferred Sarah to collar someone else Michael felt he should make the introductions. However, Sarah either ignored or wanted to ignore Ruth and before he could do so Sarah spoke.

'Michael, do come and see my father. He wants to tell you about his stint in India. You've always known him as a retiree, but his stories of life in the army are hilarious, and he's in the mood for telling them.'

Michael knew now why he had trouble finding Sarah when he had arrived. She was close to her father and always seemed to be in his thrall, unable to break away from him, even at a party. She would have been obscured by the audience that her father always wanted around him as he trotted out, once more, some of his anecdotes.

Michael could not escape talking to Colonel Traverse, or being talked to, he thought. He was not looking forward to it. He felt Sarah's rudeness to Ruth and glanced at his companion, about to make amends.

'Please don't let me keep you', said Ruth, guessing his thoughts.

'I'm sorry' he said. 'Can I call you about the tennis?'

Sarah affected a false smile and pulled Michael's sleeve as she marched him off toward her father. Ruth was left looking isolated as before, but self-contained, as if in thought. As Michael looked back at her apologetically, he had never seen anyone so attractive, her dark hair shining in the sun, the brim of her hat casting a shadow on her face like a coy veil.

The sight of Colonel Traverse startled Michael. He could not have been more surprised if the colonel had been wearing a woman's ball gown. He was wearing the black shirt, with mandarin collar that was the uniform of the British Union of Fascists. The BUF had links with Mussolini and Hitler and was led by the British aristocrat, Oswald Mosley. It even had its own Roman stiff-armed salute and an insignia of a lightning flash, reminiscent of the swastika, which was displayed prominently on the colonel's shirt sleeve.

The nasal voice of Colonel Traverse greeted him as he approached.

'So Michael, it's off to the sub continent soon.'

Colonel Traverse was tall without being imposing. Lanky was a word that came to Michael's mind. He had a large aquiline nose, which was made more prominent by being between two small, beady eyes. His gray hair was parted too far to the side of his head as if that was the way nanny had taught him how to do it. It was smoothed flat with pomade. He had a Charlie Chaplin moustache that made his upper lip look too long.

'Of course, you're in a different area of India than I was in. You're up there in the arid north. I was in Madras. Sweltering hot. First thing you notice are the smells.'

Michael noticed a smell at that moment. It was the pungent smell of cologne that the colonel must have sprayed liberally on himself before the party.

Michael did not respond, and the colonel continued.

'I'm glad you're up there, doing your bit. Teaching those natives a thing or two about freedom and democracy. Not that they're ready for it and it's little thanks we get for it, eh? You know I was out there when that Amritsar thing happened.'

'What was that?' asked Sarah.

Michael turned to her. His voice was low and serious.

'A British officer, General Dyer, ordered troops to fire into a crowd of civilians who were gathered at the Sikh temple of Amritsar. They didn't seem to know the British had banned large gatherings. Three hundred died, more than a thousand were injured.'

Traverse frowned at Michael.

'It was unfortunate, of course. But Dyer was only doing his job. Without people like him there would be mayhem. Good chap, Dyer. Knew a fellow who served under him. We actually had a collection for him in our mess at the time, and I can tell you Michael ...' the colonel wagged his finger in front of Michael's face, '... we weren't the only ones! The money went towards his defense fund. It wasn't as if the natives weren't warned.'

'It's a huge blemish on the British record,' said Michael.

Traverse's naturally florid complexion reddened still further. Michael saw his mustachioed lip moving with animation over his yellowing teeth.

'I don't think I heard that, Michael. If I did, I think you might want to retract it. You can't pussy-foot when it comes to duty in the military. You ought to know that.'

Michael felt unusually bold as he disagreed with the colonel. 'I beg to differ,'he said. 'Fact is, we lost the moral high ground after that. Winston Churchill even condemned the incident in Parliament.'

'Oh, come on, now, Michael! Churchill? That old bore? The only thing he gets right is India. He says it's no more a united nation than the Equator. Ha-Ha! Got that right, at least!'

Michael was reminded how much he disliked the colonel's mirthless laugh that always interspersed his conversation.

Michael attempted to interrupt him. 'Well, no! I ...' But the colonel was in full flow.

'But the fool thinks we ought to be arming ourselves against the Germans, now, just when Hitler's whipping his country into shape. Got 5 million off the unemployed rolls there. No, we should follow our national interests. Need more men like Hitler in this country. That's why I follow Mosley. For a greater Britain. Put people back to work.' He leaned toward Michael and hissed a whisper in his ear. 'I'm getting a lot of support, you know. Thought I would. Stroke of genius to put the uniform on today. A lot of questions asked.'

Michael could imagine the sort of questions. He glanced behind the colonel. He could see two young men whispering behind their hands as they looked at the colonel and laughed.

Everyone was aware of Mosley's rise. Mosley was a great self-publicist and had arranged big rallies in Olympia and the Albert Hall. Photographs in the papers showed crowds of men sharing the Roman salute with their leader. The Nazis managed to look menacing even in lederhosen, yet Mosley's movement looked pathetic in their home-sewn black shirts, just as Traverse looked ridiculous in the uniform – a cross between a scout master and a bus conductor, thought Michael. He felt the BUF was like an arcade-game version of the Nazi party. The colonel continued, oblivious to the bad impression he made.

'Gave those London Jews and their foreign-leaning cronies something to think about. It's our land so why shouldn't we march through the neighbourhoods they've taken over, eh? Britain for the British.'

Michael felt like grabbing the colonel by his black shirt in a throttle grip and telling him eyeball to eyeball, in graphic detail, where to put his nasty opinions. Instead he smiled in deference to his future father-in-law, and to save everyone embarrassment. Traverse cast aside his pugnacious pose and smiled to ingratiate the bystanders. Michael resented his easy dismissal of such an emotive issue.

'Had great fun in India', said Traverse, as he put one hand on his hip in what appeared to be an attempt to look debonair; the well-seasoned, jovial colonel addressing one who was still wet behind the ears. 'Fancy dress balls were the thing in the club house. One night I arrived in my costume and had a ghastly shock,' he continued. 'I suddenly realized I wasn't the only Lawrence of Arabia there. There were three of us, and one was the ruddy brigadier. D'you know what he said? 'I see we have a whole tribe of genuine Bedouins here tonight.' Ha! Ha! Bloody embarrassing!'

It was difficult to think of the colonel ever being embarrassed, thought Michael.

Traverse chuckled at his own joke as Sarah laughed a little too shrilly. Michael smiled politely and was relieved to notice his friend the vicar standing just behind their group He made his excuses to join him.

'There's Macleod, by Jove!' said Traverse on seeing the vicar. 'Better watch my *p*s and *q*s and keep the ruddy language in check! Ha! Ha!'

The Reverend Canon Macleod was wearing his clerical collar, because he was there in a semi-official capacity to support his roof fund. Michael was struck by the contrast between Traverse and Macleod, even through they were the same age. Macleod was also tall, but he had a gentleness about him that was at odds with his athletic build. He was well into his fifties, but he looked youthful for his age. His hair, although gray, was still thick, and his body was straight. His priest's shirt was black under his white linen jacket, but, he did not look somber. His disposition was too genial to ever look forbidding. Now close to retirement, he would never be promoted above the position of vicar in a small parish. But he was content with his lot, even though Michael thought he could have been a bishop, with his sharp mind and even more acute compassion. His two daughters were grown and married and they lived close by, offering him some comfort after the death of his wife four years ago.

He saw Michael approaching, and as Michael offered his hand in greeting, Macleod did something unexpected. He held his arms out and, before Michael could avoid it, he embraced him in a Russian-style bear hug. Michael smiled, whether in embarrassment or at the looks of shock on the faces of bystanders, he did not know.

'Splendid to see you, Michael! Absolutely splendid!' said Macleod.

The words might have sounded exaggerated to some, but Michael knew they were heartfelt.

'I see you're not the only one in a black shirt today, Canon Macleod' said Michael.

Macleod laughed heartily, and then checked himself. 'I shouldn't mock, should I, Michael? I mustn't cast stones. But honest to goodness, what crazy theatre is that? He looks like the man himself, that horrible Mosley character. Mosely's ideas won't catch on, though.'

'What makes you so sure?' said Michael.

'There's a British allergy to authoritarianism. After all, just think of how Cromwell refused to become king and how our Civil War was the first true revolution, don't you think? You see it in every day life, too. Just the other day I was in the train and I had a shock when I asked a man a simple question. I only asked him to close the window a little because he was sitting right by it and it would have saved me stumbling over his feet. You should have seen his reaction! He was most put out. You see, he thought I was being bossy and manipulative. He would not be dictated to. It's a typical reaction in this country.'

'So you think we have nothing to worry about and can stand back to enjoy our parties?'

Macleod looked hurt, as if Michael had offended him.

'Michael, you and I know better. Churchill is right. He said there will be an invasion of Poland and a full scale pogrom of the Jews, and there will be. How can people not see it? I agree the Treaty of Versailles was too punitive, and now they've dumped that. But meanwhile Hitler has left the League of Nations, abandoned the disarmament agreement and …' Macleod lowered his voice and leaned forward to speak in Michael's ear. '…And I have had word that they're training 7,000 pilots and that concentration camps...' Macleod suddenly stopped himself, straightened up, and quickly added, 'But that's enough of that. There are some things I have to keep to myself.'

Michael looked at him with curiosity. Macleod seemed unnervingly well-informed. There was more to the vicar than appearances revealed, and his words hinted that he was working behind the scenes with some government agency. Michael knew that Churchill was receiving information from all sorts of sources; otherwise he would not be so knowledgeable about the situation in Germany. He was convinced there was an entire network in Britain, gathering intelligence and preparing for possible war because he was an experienced soldier and recognized the value of good reconnaissance. Macleod was an unlikely looking spy, but perhaps that qualified him well for the job-that and his innate sense of justice. He used to teach Michael the verse of a favorite hymn, when Michael was still a school boy. 'Dare to be a Daniel, Dare to stand alone, Dare to have strong feelings, Dare to make them known.'

'It's so good to see you after so long and after the dreadful business with John Fairbrother', said Macleod. He suddenly looked dejected, and his eyes became moist.

'Oh Lord!' thought Michael. 'I do hope he's not going to cry!'

'His parents are ...well ... you know!' continued Macleod, his voice becoming dangerously tremulous. Michael wanted to change the subject. Macleod's visible emotions would soon become a spectacle unless he could distract him. He already saw some women looking over at Macleod, whispering as if in conspiracy and vainly trying to suppress their giggles. Macleod was known for his susceptibility to showing feelings, like the way he had spontaneously greeted Michael just now with a hug. In church he would wave his arms to rouse everyone to sing the hymns, his own voice cheerfully leading the choir at one half beat faster than the choir master's baton. The choir master was always left blinking nervously, as if the blinks would help everyone to keep up with the runaway voice of the vicar. Then there were the times when the sermon necessitated a reference to good wives and mothers, and he would mention his own departed spouse. There would then be a pause, as he calmed himself, followed by a terrific blowing of his nose into a voluminous handkerchief, a noise that sounded like a bull elephant. One friend of his mother, with the reputation of a gossip, had even sidled up to Michael after one church service and asked 'Are both his parents British?' Michael had pretended not to know whom she was talking about. 'I mean the vicar,' she insisted. 'It seems to me that he has rather foreign mannerisms. Do you know anything about his background?' When Michael said he did not, she seemed grumpy, as if thwarted in some way. 'You men are never curious enough. I think it is Italian blood or French. He's not cunning like the French, though', she mused. Michael thought the same woman was bound to be scrutinising Macleod from some corner of the garden, waiting for him to do something that she could then gossip about. He sensed the danger of Macleod's impending humiliation but, even though he stood so close to him now, Michael could think of no discreet way to calm his friend.

'His parents want to meet you soon and they have some questions,' continued Macleod. This remark made Michael even more ill-at-ease and he could guess the awkward questions the parents would ask, which he could not possibly answer, without betraying trust and revealing some secrets. 'Something about a girl' said Macleod, oblivious to Michael's discomfort. Michael finally managed to find something to say to steer the conversation in a different direction.

'Of course, I'll be returning to India soon'

'Yes. Looking forward to it?' asked Macleod.

Michael did not reveal any of his misgivings about India. He talked quickly until he was almost babbling to distract his friend. 'Oh, yes. I'm so lucky to be in my regiment. It was very competitive to get in, but it was worth it. I've now mastered Gurkhali, and have got to know and like the Gurkha ways, even their sense of humor. A frown suddenly creased Michael's brow. 'The Pathan are another story however. Ruthless, cold-blooded killers and totally irreligious.'

'Their religion may not be yours Michael, but many muslims are devout believers.'

Although he didn't consider himself irreligious and believed in God, Michael was certainly not a devout believer. At school his faith had waned after many long enforced chapel attendances and he had gradually lost interest in any organized religion. 'I'm not sure you would say that it you'd seen what I have. It's difficult to convey the life out there. You've never served overseas, have you?'

Macleod looked down and seemed to be addressing his shoes. 'I have served in the army'.

Michael's curiosity was heightened and he was briefly distracted from thoughts of Ruth, which had been constantly nagging at him like hunger pangs.

'Really, I didn't know that! Who were you with? When did you serve? You've kept this dark for a long time.'

He had known Canon Macleod for most of his life while his parents had lived in Camberley. Macleod officiated at his father's funeral, not long before he had lost his own wife. He always seemed such a reassuring domestic presence; someone who wore his heart on his sleeve and whom you felt you could trust. Macleod had progressed from the cloistered world of public school to Oxford and then into the Church. If there was one thing for which Michael could fault him, it was his sheltered life. Now he was glimpsing another side to him.

'I'll tell you about it some other time.' Macleod was uncomfortable and keen to change the subject, which only piqued Michael's curiosity more. There were mysteries in this man's life after all, something dark.

'It's clouding over. Looks like rain'. Macleod had adroitly changed the subject, using the perennial British ruse of talking about the weather.

The garden was indeed darkened by one of those gray, billowing clouds that unexpectedly punctuate the English summer sky. A drop suddenly splashed in Michael's teacup. Then another. He looked round for his cue to dash for shelter on the veranda, and with any luck find himself next to Ruth again. He would engineer another meeting, make it look like chance, but no one moved. The drops were large and sporadic. Michael looked at Colonel Traverse just in front of him. He was still continuing his monologue and had a small, gallantly patient audience, by now. Two frail, elderly sisters, the Cullens, were looking up adoringly at him. Sarah shot Michael a look, as if to reproach him for his abandoning the group.

The scene of a crowd, gamely ignoring the rain was comical to Michael, but at the same time it was admirable. Everyone stood their ground with a sense of duty and optimism that the rain would pass. It was how the civilian British reacted to war, thought Michael. They stood their ground, not surrendering an inch, waiting for the trouble to pass. Only the children ran about. They were chanting.

'It's raining, it's pouring, the old man is snoring.'

Out of the corner of his eye Michael saw a child run too close to Traverse, who then grabbed the boy's arm. The colonel mouthed a stern rebuke. The child, who was not more than seven years old, looked wide-eyed and scared, unable to break away from the fierce grip and the gruesome expression on his captor's face. The colonel shook the boy, as he held him by the scruff of his neck. When finally the child was released, he ran over to his mother and cried uncontrollably. The mother shot a disapproving look at the colonel, but he had already returned to his audience, smiling benignly. The contrast troubled Michael. The expression on the colonel's face as he caught the child had been ugly. Yet he had been able to hide his ferocity in an instant with a mask of magnanimity. For the first time Michael was seeing the colonel's hypocrisy. No one but the child's mother seemed to notice. The colonel should have been rebuked, thought Michael. But the incident seemed to pass unnoticed.

Mrs Waller appeared carrying cups of tea on a silver tray. She looked particularly short and rotund today, in a frilly apron, with one strap falling off the shoulder. She glanced up at the pesky cloud.

'Tsk, tsk! Shame!' she muttered.

But the breeze quickly shifted the cloud and the sun re-appeared. The little groups had stood their ground and not surrendered to the elements.

Mrs Rogers gave some discreet orders to Mrs Waller, who looked flustered, turning first right and then left with her tray of rattling teacups.

A small dog ran through her feet, and an expletive escaped rather too loudly from her lips.

'Bugger!'

Heads turned toward her with pre-set looks of disapproval. Such a clear expression of emotion was unsuitable, especially at a public gathering, and especially from a servant. Mr Bovis looked particularly disgruntled, with a school master's frown on his face. It was a look that he usually used to reprimand a recalcitrant clerk at bank. The swear word had interrupted a small anecdote he was recounting to an important potential client. Yet Michael found a curious comfort in her gaffe. The crowd was too sanctimonious. They needed a shake-up. Trust Mrs Waller to speak her mind! He looked at all the frowns of disapproval, and he suddenly saw Ruth close by. She had seen everything, and was the only one enjoying the joke. Their eyes met, and they smiled at each other, recognizing a shared sense of fun.

It was not just the heat that now flushed Mrs Waller's face but all the angry faces. More exasperated than ever, she rattled and clinked her way back to the French doors of the veranda, and haven of the kitchen. Michael wished he could take Ruth's hand and also disappear into the shelter of the house. He approached her.

'You look a bit lonely over here,' he said.

'No, I've been talking a lot. Too much. I think I must go home soon.'

Her German accent was stronger than before. She must be tired, thought Michael.

Michael saw her stare in Colonel Traverse's direction. She had the fierce look of a gunfighter sizing up a rival before a duel.

'Don't go yet. Please!' said Michael. Ruth did not seem to hear him as she continued to stare. Michael thought he sounded too pressing, but he persisted. 'At least come and have a cup of tea,' he said. He tried to re-capture the role of concerned host. He grasped her arm and felt a curious thrill. It was only then that she was distracted away from the sight of Traverse.

Ruth laughed. 'Why do the British always think a cup of tea will make everything better? The national elixir! Why not! Maybe a cup of tea will help sort out my life .'

As they strolled towards the refreshment table, their way was blocked by crowds and the elderly Murphy couple, who were sitting in wicker garden chairs. Mr Murphy looked dazed, his hand resting on his gold-topped cane, while Mrs Murphy was in an extraordinary pose. Her legs were akimbo under her dress, her head lolled back as if to look skywards, and her mouth was wide open. There was a loud sound of snoring. Michael looked at Ruth, not knowing whether to squeeze through and risk disturbing them. Ruth smiled and shook her head gently, silently telling Michael to leave them in peace. But suddenly Sarah appeared. She spoke loudly, waking Mrs Murphy with a start and forcing her husband out of his reverie.

'Hello, Michael. Hello, there!' she shouted.

Michael thought her cruel but stopped himself from telling her to keep her voice down. He felt a peculiar guilt about being found with Ruth.

'Michael, where on earth have you been?' Sarah asked. 'Peter, Vera and I want to go to the country pub I told you about. It's open now, and we wanted you to drive us there. Let's get going, shall we?'

She was angry and ignored Ruth.

'I don't think mum can spare me,' said Michael.

'Yes', said Sarah triumphantly. 'I just asked her if we could steal you, and she was only too happy to do so.'

He saw it all. His mother was championing Sarah at every opportunity. He could hear her say, 'Such a nice girl, Michael. Good parents and I believe the Traverse family have quite a bit tucked away. Some aged, childless aunt had married a wealthy gentleman in the City, and has left them a small fortune.'

He turned to his new neighbour. 'I'd better go, Ruth. I'll be in touch.'

Sarah glanced at Ruth and pulled at Michael's sleeve, her lips slightly pursed. Without saying anything, Ruth turned and walked away,

Sarah spoke forcefully. 'She's gone. Forget it. I'll tell you about her later. Let's just say *that* friendship is a non-starter, all right?' She then smiled to soften the well-aimed blow and led him to the driveway.

CHAPTER 3

IT WAS LAUGHABLE when she found time to laugh. The German Jewish refugee in the most conservative of British towns. A community that had grown like a coral from the bed of the officer training college. All the officers flocked to it for a taste of home while on leave and to use it for a haven for their memsahibs who wanted to give birth away from the medical terrors of the tropics. There was a lot of fading away of old soldiers in Camberley as they sat in each others drawing rooms, swathed in cigar smoke and the droning sound of oft-repeated anecdotes. Camberley was reassuring. Like minds comfortingly confirming prejudices. Newcomers were at best disconcerting and they could be threatening. The herd instinct ruled and its solidarity made up for the lack of old world charm of the town. Even the local church was an ersatz Tudor concoction, the sort of make-believe Englishness seen in the hill stations of British India.

So Ruth was truly the outsider even though she was living with her grandmother who had been there for forty years, and even though she had visited her so frequently from her childhood. Ruth's grandmother was seen as someone on the margins of the society. It was strange, people thought, that she had not chosen a stockbroker's traditional suburb, like Reigate, where there was a Jewish community. There were, of course, Jewish army officers in the town, but if they kept Jewish traditions, they did so discreetly. Ruth's grandmother was proud of her heritage, and openly celebrated many traditions and holidays but she preferred to live away from the peer pressures of a Jewish community. Perhaps there was something in Ruth that was like her grandmother, a refusal to accept authority unquestioningly and a mind always searching for challenging new ideas.

Ruth had always bucked the system. Her parents had long predicted trouble for her and they had not even counted on the alarming rise in anti-Semitism in Germany. It was inescapable in their home city, Berlin, even though it did have the largest population of Jews in Germany. By

1930 even to be Jewish seemed to be an admission of insurrection. Ruth was an accident waiting to happen – a word, a gesture would always escape her when provoked. She did not know when to be quiet. She did not even learn from her brother Heinrich, who had only recently escaped death by a whisker. He had told her of a terrifying incident as a warning.

'So imagine me there on the train, Ruth. I'm in the fourth class compartment.'

'Well, if you will travel cheaply, Heinrich…' Ruth interrupted, adopting the bantering tone she always used with her brother.

'No. I'm serious, Ruth. There are four surly youths with me in the compartment. Suddenly the lights go out. "Goddam Jews!" says one loudly. He has to speak above the noise of the rattling rails. "They're to blame." "Yeah, they betrayed the Fatherland. They betray us." I listen in silence until I just can't take any more. I find myself saying, "I am a Jew and a patriot. And I'm proud of it". They laugh sneeringly. I can't stop myself. "My father fought in the Great War for Germany. He risked his life for his country. One in five Jews who fought never came back." "That was one way to get rid of them" says the biggest lout. "Seems like the Jew wants to argue", says his friend. "And what do we do with upstart Jewish boys?" The response is chilling. It comes from the darkest corner. "We throw him from the train". I quickly shut my mouth, Ruth, I knew I should never had said anything. I get a hot feeling in my stomach. Never, ever be as stupid as me. Keep quiet.'

Ruth looked at her brother. 'You were all right though,' she said with only a hint of nervousness in her voice.

'Luckily I was. Their drunken, cackling laughter seemed to break the tension, and the darkness hid me, their target. But I learned my lesson.'

'You exaggerate, Heinrich,' said Ruth. 'They would have baited you even if you weren't Jewish.'

Heinrich shook his head, either to deny it or in resignation at his sister's reaction. She was always stubborn.

Ruth's parents knew there would be a crisis early in her life. Close friends could not understand their nervousness. Ruth seemed the conventional daughter. She dressed conservatively, was polite, did well at school. She even played the piano beautifully, which showed how she could focus on serious studies. But her parents knew that that same focus was the cause of her problems. She was stubborn and found it difficult to change her mind, or to listen to her elders. When she decided on something it was very difficult to dissuade her.

The same fault, the strong-mindedness, made her fiercely loyal. If her family criticised any of her friends she would speak up for them and never accept the barbs. She would speak out about politics, injustices, just the sort of things that would put her in harm's way in fascist Germany, as Heinrich had feared.

Her friend Greta had warned her parents of a worrying incident and it confirmed for the parents the basis of their anxiety for her. It had taken place at a fashionable venue – the terrace of the Café Mozart. Unfortunately, loutish young national socialists – the sort that had been on Heinrich's train – had taken to lolling there. They would never have dared to frequent the place before. Customer disapproval and the waiter's admonitions would have chased them away. Now they sensed their invulnerability and were determined to enjoy it. Seeing the helpless indignation of the customers made their stake-out more enjoyable.

Ruth and Greta were drinking their coffee and savoring their cream cakes. The two young men were smoking and talking too loudly at an adjoining table. Greta and Ruth reacted by watching and giggling at their oafishness, whispering to one another. Then one young man got up and lumbered towards their table. He seemed to puff himself up like one of those big gorillas at the zoo. He suddenly seized a chair at their table and sat down. He leaned across the table, his spotty face loomed up against theirs, his breath smelt of beer. 'Share the joke, ladies', he said. Normally some older woman or the café staff would have intervened. But they just glanced nervously towards them and looked away again. Greta saw Ruth's eyes narrow. She knew her friend was about to come out with a withering comment and had to act quickly. She saw the danger all too clearly. 'I've seen those types before, Mrs Goldberg,' she told

Ruth's mother. 'I've seen them rough people up, humiliate them. I've even seen them pick on children, who were too terrified to cry.'

Clara Goldberg nodded sadly. 'But I knew what to do. I just smiled and told Ruth we were late, dragging her by the hand before she could say anything. There was a catch, though.'

'Ach, there's more?' said Clara in exasperation.

'The young man said, 'Ruth? That's an unusual name. Not Jewish are you?' I laughed and said 'O, no! Just a family name. She's half English, you know!' I dragged her away to hear him saying, 'Wonderful! You're half English and I'm half drunk.' Mrs Goldberg, if I hadn't been there I dread to think what would have happened to Ruth'.

Clara could only smile to mask her fears. 'Thank you for telling me, Greta' she said. She already knew of the dangers in the streets and public places. Their lives were becoming ever more tyrannised. There was only one compensation, though a very poor one, that the Goldberg parents could not even acknowledge to themselves. It would help them with a family crisis Ruth was about to unleash on them. The usual trials of life paled in comparison to the dangers of living as a Jew under the looming shadow of Adolf Hitler.

The problem began with Ruth falling in love with the same intensity she had for everything close to her heart. Ruth had begun her studies at the university, which she hoped would enable her to become a medical doctor. There she had met a handsome young man about whom she could not keep quiet. He was not Jewish and this would normally have disappointed her parents, though not irrevocably. They were not very religious though they frequently celebrated Shabbat, with the lighting of candles, prayers, meal on a Friday night. They also kept the Jewish holidays. They believed in the integrity of their community and cherished the traditions that had passed down to them for thousands of years. They wanted to pass the baton to the next generation. They were prepared however, to respect the independence of their children, as they had seen some of their friends do. But this young man Ruth favoured unsettled them for other reasons. He was older than Ruth by seven years and so youth could not excuse his bad manners. He was too forthright, talking as if he were holding court, and always about himself – his journeys around Europe in his car, the time he was entertained by Baron von X or General von Y, the practical jokes he had played when he had had too much beer.

'So there we were, celebrating the night before my friend Franz's wedding and I had a brilliant idea. Why not strip him stark naked and leave him on the country road in the dark. You should have seen the look on his face as we left him there. Like a *Kindergartner* left by his mother for the first time. It was hilarious.'

He would laugh loudly at his own jokes. It was not respectful. True, he was very handsome, but this seemed to give him too much confidence. He seemed to flirt with any woman in the room, whether young or old. Clara was convinced he even tried to flirt with her, having the bad manners to compliment her on her dress or hairstyle or teasing the maid when she brought in the coffee. 'Fraulein, is that a blush I see on your face. What are you hiding? Thoughts of your paramour, eh?'

Ruth was unusually silent when he was around, though she laughed at his jokes and nodded encouragingly at his stories. Clara watched Ruth anxiously before one of his visits to the house. She would fuss nervously, plumping up the cushions in the drawing room, going to the kitchen to inspect the snack that cook had prepared with the coffee. She had a certain sparkle in her eyes since meeting Rainer, and her appetite had diminished. She showed an unusual impatience to arrive early for lectures at the same university that Rainer, the eternal student, it seemed, was attending. Clara had tried to warn her daughter.

'A handsome German aristocrat, Ruth, who clearly enjoys having women at his feet. What do you think he wants with my pretty young Jewish daughter?'

Ruth became heated when she heard such comments. 'You have no idea. You're just like anyone else of your generation, and you always bring this Jewish thing in. We're more enlightened than when you were young.'

Her mother's warnings became more urgent. 'He's up to no good. You must never be alone with him, Ruth.'

Finally Ruth's parents limited the evenings out that she was allowed. But how could they regulate her time at the university? How could they monitor the hikes she took with her friends in the mountains, when they knew that Rainer was among them? How could they influence her when, contrary to them, she admired the way he could commandeer an audience, and shrugged off the coterie of women that surrounded him, accepting it as confirmation of his attractiveness.

Clara and her husband could only hint at another side of Rainer that made them anxious. He was well-connected with the German establishment, and spoke of friends who were known as National Socialist sympathisers. For all his talk, Rainer seemed the type who would, in the end, blow with the prevailing wind. If that meant backing fascists, so be it! That was the opinion of both parents, when they discussed him behind the bedroom doors.

Ruth was immune to the hints of this darker side to the man. On the contrary, she saw in Rainer a maverick spirit like her own. After all, he laughed at the fascists; he made fun of their stupid catch-phrases.

Ruth loved what she saw as the rebel in Rainer. When they were hiking in the mountain with friends he would sidle up and say to her, 'Let's just run away. Let's lose the others, take a different trail.'

And then they did, walking off together, giving the others a vague excuse of taking a photograph of a certain view, or looking for a more rugged route as a challenge. Ruth's mood became as vertiginous as some of the drops beneath the narrow paths. Then, when clambering up a steep rocky slope, Rainer had reached for her hand. It happened so quickly, the thrill of his warm, firm grasp. And then they could not let go when the path became more even. It was an awakening for Ruth. How quickly did holding hands progress to an embrace, to warm urgent lips pressing against hers in the flower-filled alpine meadows, hands now moving all over her in sinuous movements. She felt an abandon like when she had once drunk too much. The empty pastures around her felt part of her as she felt the dry soft grass under her back, still warm from the sunshine. The shielding veil of the nearby forest sheltered her. The hard threatening streets of the city were a world away, as the breeze tousled her partner's light-filled hair and she drew his head towards her for another kiss. His laughter was caught by the same winds and it seemed to be carried in circles around her. No need now for fancy words, for hand-on-heart commitments to seduce the young woman.

It was afterwards that Ruth wanted the declarations of love, the tenderness. But she would not ask for them. She was too proud. She may have changed in a way, wanting a sign of commitment from him, but he had not changed. He became, if anything, more light-hearted, and keener to stay with the group. There was no more talk of running away.

Ruth sought the advice of her friend Greta.

'I don't understand it. One minute he was talking about running away with me and then he seems to be running away from me. What's the matter with him?' She did not want to tell her friend about the incident in the mountain meadows.

'Then,' she continued, 'when I had a chance in the pub at lunchtime, I whispered to him, 'when can we see each other again?' He just smiled and said, 'Soon! Soon!' He didn't even bother to whisper.'

Greta had bad news for Ruth.

'You know he's going away, don't you?

'Going away? Where? Why' said Ruth , before she could mask the panic in her voice, and the sharp stab of shock in her stomach.

'He's going to Munich to do some more studies. Didn't he tell you?'

'O yes, yes! I think he did.' It was unusual for Ruth to lie. 'He didn't want to go into details. Didn't want to disappoint me. He's very considerate like that.'

'Mmm!' answered Greta, distractedly.

So that is why he has been so offhand with me, thought Ruth. He is afraid of upsetting me.

Rainer left shortly afterwards, knowing, said Greta, that another circle of admirers waited for him in Munich.

At home Clara noticed that Ruth had become unusually withdrawn, spending hours in her bedroom, rising late in the morning just before her lectures, and appearing with the swollen eyes of one who had been crying all night.

She could not keep her pregnancy secret from her mother. Clara was at first shocked and panic-stricken. But Clara was a practical woman and a protective mother. Her English upbringing had given her a calm stoical side. She told Ruth she would approach her father.

'Now don't worry if he becomes very angry and upset, Ruth. He'll find a way of coping. Of coping for all of us. Don't worry.'

Dr Goldberg had reacted remarkably calmly to his wife's news, as one who is already beleaguered with worries. He was an able man and he consulted lawyer friends and civil servants. He then insisted on going to Munich by himself to meet Rainer.

'No, you can't do that, papa. I haven't even told him. I don't want him to know. Please, please don't do that! Stop him Mutti! It will ruin everything.'

'He must be made to face his responsibilities,' said her father firmly.

Ruth made every excuse for Rainer. 'He's looking after his family. His mother is sick. He has his exams coming up. We can't tell him. Not yet'

'We do not have time on our hands. I am your father. I will look after you' said Dr Goldberg.

'I don't want him to feel trapped. I don't want you to put a gun to his head'

Dr Goldberg became impatient and angry, having shown such restraint up until then. Perhaps the thought of guns put to heads had especially upset him in this time when innocent men, men he knew and respected, were frog-marched to the concentration camps.

'No one is putting a gun to anyone's head, you foolish girl. I will hear no more about it. My mind is made up'

Ruth fled to her bedroom in tears.

Dr Goldberg went to Munich. Somehow a civil marriage was arranged but still Rainer did not communicate with Ruth directly, and her father did not tell her of the bargain he had made with his future son-in- law. The thought of such a relationship with that man made him want to choke. But he needed the ceremony to take place and worried the Rainer would not keep his word.

Ruth blamed her parents for not hearing from Rainer. In her mind they were tearing up his letters, pretending the flowers that sometimes came to the house were ordered by themselves, telling the servants to cut off his telephone calls. She lurched from anger to inconsolable tears, and locked her bedroom door against her worried mother. Yet she still managed to attend her morning lectures, to dress up attractively, to accept Greta's kindness and comforting words whenever she confided in her.

The day of the civil ceremony approached. Ruth became strangely stoical. She had faith that Rainer would make up for his neglect, which was, after all, understandable. Clara took her daughter out, silently, joylessly, to choose a pretty white suit with matching hat and long white gloves for the ceremony. Her mother's heart felt the conflicting tugs of happiness and sadness to see her daughter looking so beautiful in white.

Then Rainer arrived, and visited Ruth's house with his Friend, Wolfgang, with whom he was staying, a bookish-looking young man, with thick horn-rimmed glasses and an unwillingness to talk. He seemed to know his presence was merely a shield between Rainer and the Goldbergs. Rainer sat on the edge of the sofa, laughing at every opportunity. At one stage he glanced up at a Rubenesque oil painting on the wall. 'If I had a woman with breasts like those, I would never leave her,' he said. His laughter drowned out the sharp intake of breath that Clara made. Ruth had no reaction. She was perplexed, preoccupied, looking for a sign from Rainer, but he glanced away quickly whenever he caught her gaze.

The civil ceremony was quick and there was only a small gathering of close family. Rainer only had two male friends to witness his vows. Pictures were taken by Heinrich on the steps of the civic building, and Ruth, either through loyalty or through her innate ability to make the best of things, would always keep the small picture in a silver frame on her dresser, a handsome couple, smiling thinly and looking at the camera rather than each other.

The small reception was held in Ruth's home, and still she waited, silently and numbly for a sign from Rainer. But Rainer left, as soon as the last guest had gone, giving her a brief peck on the cheek, and Ruth stoically resigned herself to accepting his departure in silence. His last words to her were cryptic. 'It will all be all right', he had said. She ran to her bedroom and flung herself on the bed to cry. The sobs and moans were loud and irrepressible. Clara silently came into the room and sat next to the prostrate figure. She stroked her daughter's hair. 'My baby! My baby!' Ruth suddenly turned and flung her arms around her mother's neck. She smelt her mother's familiar lavender perfume as she buried her face in the soft silky blouse, just as she had used to do as a child when she was upset.

'It's unfair, Mutti. It's so unfair'

If she had looked at her mother, she would have seen she had the face of one of those martyrs in medieval paintings.

'We know unfairness, Ruth. We know cruelty. That's our history, our legacy. But look! We've survived.'

The memory of those words would later haunt Ruth.

'Look! I have something for you,' said Clara.

She produced a package in delicate tissue paper and tied with a white satin ribbon.

'It might not seem like much of a wedding gift, but it's more precious to me than any of the finest Fabergé jewellery you could find. Like Fabergé, it comes from Russia'

Ruth sat up and wiped her wet face with the palm of her hand. She carefully took the small package, gently untying the ribbon. There was an old piece of white silk. The fact that it was yellowing with age did not matter. You could see the colourful and beautiful embroidery. It was a yarmulke, the sort that would have been used by a groom on his wedding day.

'This was made by one of your great, great grandmothers in Russia. It was made with great care, and, I like to think, with love. It has come down to us through generations of mothers, and now it is yours'

Ruth smiled at last and held it close to her.

'I will treasure it, Mutti'. She kissed her mother.

Clara did not know how Ruth would or could recover, in spite of seeing such brief moments of cheerfulness. Her daughter was like one in mourning for the next month. She walked through the streets of Berlin, looking for Rainer's face in the crowd. She listened dolefully to love songs in the cafes, where Greta met her and did her best to comfort her.

Then, one day, it suddenly changed. Ruth was sitting with Greta on the sofa at home, when she suddenly felt a strange stirring in her stomach. At first she thought it was indigestion, but then, when the sensation repeated itself, she knew it was her baby. She smiled and her natural ebullience welled up in her again.

Greta! Greta! I felt the baby! I did!'

There was no shame, no regret – only joy.

Plans were made. Her pregnancy was not obvious, and six weeks before the baby was due, she was to go to a private clinic in Bavaria, where she would give birth. She would then travel to England with the child, to escape the hothouse of gossip of Berlin society and the growing threats to Jews in Germany.

And Rainer? Dr Goldberg's plan would now come into play. After the birth, the marriage would be quickly and quietly annulled. Ruth, with her strangely generous nature, had forgiven her 'husband' and told her parents, much to their disapproval, that she would keep in touch with him and allow him to see the child on visits to Germany. Her headiness at the birth of her child and the ability to shrug off criticism gave her strength. Even she did not know whether it was the effects of pregnancy that made her serene or just a happy coincidence of character. She had become wiser, but not cynical. Her thirst to live for the moment was, if anything, heightened by her pregnancy and by events in Germany.

'I'm worried about this clinic,' said Clara. 'What happens when they realise the father is not around? What happens when they learn you are a Jew? It's in Bavaria, for God's sake. We should have gone to Switzerland.'

'O Mutti! Where is that English *sang froid* of yours? Everything will be fine.'

The time came. Ruth and her mother were walking on a small path in the mountain village where the clinic was situated. They were beside a loud mountain stream, the shallow waters gushing white beside them. Suddenly Ruth felt the pains, sharp clenchings in her stomach. She felt the damp flow of her waters breaking and leaned heavily on her mother's arm.

'We have to go quickly mother.' She hobbled back up the path with Clara encouraging her to stay calm, stopping every few minutes and stooping as a wave of pain ebbed and flowed through her.

The labour was quick, and the pain blotted out all thoughts as she repeated the mantra to herself. 'I will see my baby soon. Soon I will see the baby.' The excitement and encouragement of the attendants grew until Ruth felt a sudden release and lightening as the baby appeared and announced his demand for attention with loud wailing.

'It's a boy. A beautiful boy!' said Clara. She kissed her daughter's forehead before taking the small child, newly cleaned, from the nurse and handing him to Ruth. Ruth nuzzled the warm, red little face, and the head, fuzzy with sparse, dark hair. She laughed, with tears in her eyes and gently opened the blanket to see the tiny form, the little nipples, the tiny fingers, curling and uncurling with the perfectly-formed nails, pink like little shells.

Later, Ruth would look back on her time in the clinic with happiness. It was only after many years that it was tinged with sadness. She had met another young mother in the clinic, who had just given birth to her first child, a daughter. A quiet, and friendly woman, Ruth had discovered that she too was Jewish, and that her husband was a doctor in Frankfurt. They had shared the first joys of motherhood and Ruth had kept in touch until communication was impossible. Then, later, she had tried to find her, but there was no trace of her or her relatives. It was obvious that she and her family were among the victims of Hitler's Germany, that proud, plump-faced mother with her funny Yiddish references and sayings, that she had whispered quietly to Ruth, knowing the stigma they could lead to, and her tiny, treasured baby.

CHAPTER 4

MICHAEL WAS DEEP IN THOUGHT as he drove his mother's Morris Oxford with Sarah beside him in the passenger seat, which he found uncomfortably intimate. Vera cozied up to Peter in the back. Sarah was expecting him to set the wedding date today. He hoped that this would put to rest the uncertainties and anxieties that were eating away at him. After all, he thought, Sarah was good fun and vivacious, even if she was bossy and gauche at times. He could see her making a perfect regimental wife, unfazed by the rigors and privations of life in a hill station. He wondered what she had meant about Ruth being a 'non-starter'. Surely she could not think he had any designs on her. Even knowing what he did about her, there were too many obstacles to a close friendship. She was Jewish, she had a child, maybe even a husband back in Germany, her family would not approve of him, and he was returning to India in a few weeks. Still, she was attractive, and he could allow himself a discreet flirtation, without being disloyal to Sarah.

The fresh evening air blew through the open windows, and tousled the girls' hair, now that they had discarded their hats. They had to talk loudly over the noise of the engine, which seemed to add to their excitement. Vera leaned forward and whispered to Sarah who laughed loudly and told her to be quiet, while giving Michael a sideways look. They were conspiring about something. Vera was now regaling them with one of her anecdotes. It was supposed to be about an incident that had deeply embarrassed her, yet she did not seem to be in the least abashed as she related the details. Her mother had hosted a drinks party and Vera had been drawn towards one of the guests, a tall, handsome young man from Boston. She had flirted with him, but he had seemed a cold fish and kept shifting his gaze from her, when she gushed in admiration of America.

'I couldn't see the gaffe I was making. I just thought 'darn foreigner', but – give me credit – I did persist,' said Vera. 'I told him how I loved the accent, so manly, just like Douglas Fairbanks. The stupid man looked terribly uncomfortable and when I said 'You must be used to tea parties (my little joke – you know, the Boston Tea Party), he started to look round frantically as if he wanted someone else to talk to.'

'What on earth was wrong with the man?' said Sarah. 'Any decent chap would enjoy being cornered by a girl like you.'

'Well, I hadn't cottoned on that he was from Boston, Lancashire, not from America at all.'

They all laughed.

'He probably thought I was taking a dig at his northern accent.'

'I expect he felt like a fish out of water in Camberley. It's not an easy place for newcomers.' said Sarah. Her comment seemed pointed, and Michael thought of Ruth. 'I don't think he took offence at you Vera,' she added.

Michael suddenly felt his mood lift although it wasn't Vera's anecdote that had helped. With her quip about foreigners Michael had been reminded of the distrust of foreigners in his home town that amounted to xenophobia. A picture of Ruth had come into his mind, standing aloof in her silk dress in his mother's garden. No, he felt cheered by something that had insinuated itself into the fresh air rushing through the windows and into the sound of his friends' laughter. It was coming, too, from the familiar countryside, with the sun-dappled meadows, the ripened corn fields tinged red with poppies, the bursts of color from the yellow buttercups, and the red sorrel. Then he recognised the source of his optimism. It was the memory of his father. He had just crested a hill with a distinctive little copse at its peak which he remembered from the road trips he took with his father. He had only been a schoolboy but they had long talks together on the journeys, man to man – how Michael was getting on at school, what he would study in the top form, who was on the cricket team with him. It did not matter what the subject was, it was the shared closeness, just him and his father in the little bumpy Austin 11, as the car crested hill after hill. His father seemed to be there now, in the crowded car.

His father had been dead for four years, and at his funeral he had suddenly felt there was no buffer between him and old age any more. Yet he realised that his father had given him the confidence to face the difficulties of adult life. He was able now to focus on his responsibilities – his army career, marriage to a suitable girl like Sarah, perhaps a boy of his own, sitting next to him in the car, topping the same hills. He hoped the change in his mood would last, and that the effects of combat and what he had seen in India would no longer torment him. He knew his mother was anxious to see him being what she said was 'his old self'.

When Peter spoke up, Michael could see that he was also thinking about the future, and marriage. He had some intriguing news.

'I've just heard some gossip from that fellow officer of yours, William Jones. He can't stop talking when he's on leave, can he? You'd better not give him any cause to blabber about you!' Michael wondered if Peter was thinking about anything in particular, but he dismissed the thought. He had been blameless, unless Jones was going to resurrect the talk of that one liaison he had while on leave at a hill station. 'He says it looks like your colonel-in-chief wants to marry a divorcee.'

'Good luck to him!' said Michael.

'It's not as simple as that. All the senior officers are against it. They're saying it goes against the grain for such an emblem of the regiment to marry a divorcee, that there could be no blessing from the church, that no one would accept such a bad example, you know how it goes!'

Michael's anger surged, unstoppable. He raised his voice until he was almost shouting. 'How ridiculous! What right have they to interfere? His choice of wife doesn't reflect on him or his career, for God's sake.' His friends looked at him in silence and he reddened, realising he had over-reacted. He did not want anyone to probe too deeply into his feelings, asking too many questions. Such outbursts might lead to gossip about his state of mind. He tried to explain his reaction to the news.

'It's just that I've seen so much unhappiness lately. John Fairbrother's death. I think people should be given a chance of happiness. What do the junior officers say?'

'Like you, they think it's nobody's business but their own. They're from a younger generation.'

Michael knew what the outcome would be. 'The senior officers will have their way. The poor chap will have to resign his commission.' he said.

Sarah could not resist giving her opinion. She was talking loudly over the noise of the car and Michael felt she was bellowing in his ear. 'I think it's only right. How can you have an officer with a marriage not sanctioned by the church? It's not really a marriage at all.'

'A lot of people agree with you, Sarah,' said Michael. 'I just think it's too harsh. Just because the poor woman made a mistake, why does she have to suffer for the rest of her life?'

'I suppose you believe in easy divorce, too, and in being soft on un-married mothers' said Sarah. She gave Michael one of her 'significant' looks and he knew she was referring to Ruth. 'Admit it! You believe in giving a charter for loose women to flit from man to man.'

'No', said Michael. 'A woman who has made mistakes should not have to commit a sort of suttee and sacrifice herself to appear faithful to one man.'

'What's suttee, for heaven's sake?' asked Sarah.

'It's when Indian widows have to burn themselves on their husbands' funeral pyres. It's the ultimate test of the wife's loyalty. Of course you could turn the tables and see it as the ultimate test of disloyalty on the part of all the woman's relatives, who leave her to her fate,' said Michael. 'It was outlawed by the British in the early 1800s, but it still goes on.'

'How appalling!' said Sarah.

Vera now took an interest in the conversation. 'You've never seen it though?' she asked. Michael glanced at her in the rearview mirror. She looked as if she hoped he had been a witness to it.

Michael had seen suttee. He had been traumatised by the spectacle and he felt compelled to tell his friends the story as if, somehow, it would give them a glimpse of the other world he lived in. He gazed at the road ahead as he spoke, and his friends leaned towards him, listening intently above the noise of the engine. A funeral procession was being led by a young woman, he began, but there was something sinister about it. The young woman was strangely disheveled, in spite of her laced sari. Her large black eyes stared blankly ahead. He knew something strange was about to happen. She had the scarlet spot on her forehead, indicating her husband was still alive, but he was dead and it was his body that was carried forward by the jostling crowd. The mob were like excited spectators, hurrying towards a game, some were even grinning and laughing. Then he realized what was happening. The sad young woman was on her way to burn herself to death on her husband's funeral pyre, in spite of the ban on such a practice.

Sarah broke in. 'Stop, you're making all this up.'

'I'm not. It's been documented. It was investigated.'

'Didn't anyone stop her?' asked Vera.

'A male relative stepped in to shake her by the shoulders, to stop her and make her see sense.'

'So everything was fine', said Vera, hopefully.

'The other relatives shouted at him and dragged him off. Imagine! He was the only one out of that entire crowd who tried to save her life. The only one who tried to stop the madness. She was quickly bound, hand and foot, and set on the pyre with the old man's, her husband's, corpse.

'I don't think I want to hear the rest,' said Vera.

'No, you don't,' said Michael. 'I will never forget the screams, as I left, as quickly as possible. I couldn't see any more and I tried, with some other officers, to raise the alarm, and to get some help.'

'What a dreadful story,' said Sarah. 'It's really in very poor taste, Michael. Can't they do anything, the authorities? They should act when they see something wrong.'

Sarah had a pitiful trust in 'authorities', thought Michael. He said, 'They try, but they have to choose their battles, and this was not the time. Some token arrests were made, I believe, but the practice has not been eradicated to this day.'

Sarah was scornful. 'What barbarians!' she said.

'Sarah', said Peter, 'don't you know the Vikings, your ancestors and mine, had the same custom. You are going to find a lot to admire about India.'

'Rubbish,' said Sarah. 'There's nothing barbaric about the British, past or present'.

Michael began to think this was not going to be the day to set the wedding date. Sarah was irritating him. 'Tell that to the Chinese victims of the opium war', he said.

'I don't know much about history, but I'm surprised at you, Michael,' said Sarah. 'Anyone would think you unpatriotic.'

'Not at all,' said Michael. 'I just refuse to see things in black and white.'

'No, said Sarah. 'You just see things in black.' But we'll make you see things differently by the end of the evening, won't we Vera?' She turned around to look at her friend and they both started to giggle. Michael wondered how much longer he could suppress his negative feelings about Sarah. The evening was not going to end well, he thought.

They had reached the pub by now, which had the look of a large cottage, with its thatched roof. The light was already beginning to fade and lights glowed in welcome from the windows. They were relieved to break away from the somber conversation.

Michael smiled to himself as he watched Vera totter unsteadily over the rough driveway in high heels and a tight-fitting dress. She always tried to look fashionable, he thought, and yet her lips were a little too red, and the dark hair was too crowded with jet ornaments. It was she who lightened the mood immediately as they sat down. She began telling her friends about a recent trip with her mother to a London department store, where the poor service had shocked her.

'The old bat behind the counter asked me my dress size. I said eight. 'No', she retorted. 'You're ten'. The cheek! Then, just to humiliate me, she produced a tape measure.'

'That must have been frightful', said Sarah. 'But what else can you expect from someone with no breeding? So insensitive!'

'Well, it was frightful. But do you know the worst?'

Sarah now looked bored. 'I can't imagine', she said.

'She was right! I bought a lovely dress but Lord knows how I've put on weight! I do wish I had a figure like that new neighbour, what is her name? Ruth! She cuts quite a dash.'

Sarah looked askance at Michael and spoke loudly, as if in anger or nervousness. 'Michael, you seem to have been quite taken with Ruth.' She smiled but there was a trace of pique in her voice. 'India must be giving him a taste for the exotic!'

Michael's answer was sudden and loud. 'That's ridiculous!' His outburst took him by surprise in the same way he had been startled by his own response to Tim's news about the colonel's marriage. As he glanced at Sarah, she seemed unperturbed and he thought she even looked smug. He cleared his throat nervously and softened his voice. He was already trying to excuse himself. Sarah always made him feel apologetic about everything-about a disappointing film they had seen, the tea a waitress slopped in her saucer, the inclement weather on a recent picnic with their friends.

'I've only just met her. She looked isolated, that's all. No one else was talking to her.'

'Someone else is going to be isolated before long, aren't they, Vera?' said Sarah, and both girls started to giggle again. 'But we'll take your word for it Michael,' she continued. 'Without your attention she would have been the lonely little waif and stray.'

Sarah stiffened into her school ma'am pose. 'Well don't get too chummy! She has a child, you know. A boy of eight.'

Michael already knew this and could look unsurprised. Yet he wanted to know more. Who was the father of the child? Was he still around? Why had she left Germany so recently?

Sarah waited in silence, hoping Michael would ask her more, and she frowned when Vera interrupted, still thinking about her shopping trip.

'But the shoes weren't right, were they, Sarah? I mean the crocodile bag was just perfect. You could see the little snout down the middle and its eyes at the top, nearer the snap. But the shoes just looked common. Too chunky. The sort of shoes a young housemaid would go out in.'

Sarah had an idea. 'Shopping!' she said. 'That would be a fun outing. We could all go up to London and choose neckties at Harrods for these two fashion neophytes.'

'Neo-fighters, you mean', said Vera, laughing at her own joke.

Michael knew Sarah expected him to take up her suggestion with enthusiasm, but he stayed silent. He saw Peter squeeze Vera's hand under the table as they looked at each other. Sarah saw it too, and edged closer to Michael. He suddenly stood up.

'I think I'd better go home and help with the cleaning up.'

'Oh, Lord! Duty calls again,' said Sarah. 'You really do have a very proper streak in you, Michael. You should let your hair down, once in a while. Here, fetch some more cider.'

Michael briefly relished the idea of leaving her stranded at the pub, but he dutifully obeyed her order. It was curious how Sarah's question about Ruth had had the opposite effect to that which she had intended, he thought. It had stirred up his curiosity about the young woman and had made him conscious of how often he had been thinking of her.

He returned from the bar with a tray of drinks. But he was puzzled. His friends were no longer at the table. 'Where the devil are they?' he thought. It would be odd if they had all gone to the cloakrooms at the same time. He put down the tray of drinks and sat uneasily on the oak bench he had just been sharing with Sarah. The girls had not even left their bags. He felt more and more uncomfortable and finally decided to see if they had gone to cool off in the evening air. The night outside was refreshing and the pinpricks of bright starlight appeared between the moving wisps of clouds, luminous in the moonlight. There was silence apart from the distant laughter and mumblings of strangers. It was a setting that he could normally have enjoyed. Michael looked for his car, but what he saw was an empty spot on the gravel driveway where it had been parked. He was confused. He reached into his jacket pocket for the car keys, but they were gone. Then he realized. His friends had taken his car and had left him stranded. His heart sank. 'What a damn nuisance!' he said to himself. He decided to console himself with another beer, and sat down once more on the same bench. He felt betrayed and alone. He would have to spend the night at this inn now.

The time passed slowly and the conversation of others echoed in his ears. Each outburst of laughter made him jumpy. He was angry and thought of the words he would say to his friends when they finally met up again. 'If that's your idea of a joke...' or 'Don't you think that was a childish prank?'

Just as he was about to approach the bar to enquire about a room, Vera, Peter and Sarah came through the door towards him. The girls almost seemed to be skipping and they were laughing, and pointing at him. Only Peter seemed uneasy, glancing at him from a down turned face.

'Ha! Ha! We fooled you. Admit it!' said Sarah. 'You thought you had been abandoned. Left in the deep, dark countryside like a waif and stray!'

Michael felt betrayed and angry and his face showed it.

Sarah softened a little. 'It's not as bad as all that, Michael' said Sarah, going up to him and linking her arm with his. 'I'm sorry. I thought you'd see the joke. I just didn't want you to go back early.'

'I think we had better go home,' said Michael.

'Wouldn't you like another drink?' said Peter.

'No, let's just get on the road.'

'Alright, let's go then. We have important things to do tomorrow,' said Sarah, tapping her ring finger and looking at Michael.

Michael did not answer as he led the way to the car, the girls following and laughing. He felt very tired, and he thought once more about his father, but his time he only felt a sense of loss. He tried to steer his thoughts away from sadness, and reflected on what had amused him at the garden party – Macleod's sudden bear hug. Children's laughter. The ladies of the parish secretly quaffing sherry. Then there was Ruth. His mind could rest there if he wanted to be more cheerful. Sarah's joke had eroded any sense of guilt about savoring the thought of that pretty woman. He would have no qualms about meeting her again.

CHAPTER 5

'Mother, I wondered if you could give me Mrs. Weinstein's number? You see, I thought I'd give Ruth a call. I promised her a game of tennis.'

Michael was sitting with his mother at the breakfast table. Light poured in from the French windows and it seemed a perfect day for tennis.

Gladys put her tea cup down with a ringing clink.

'Michael, dear, do you think that's wise? You know she has a young son, and I've heard something else. The boy's father is some sort of a dark character. Mrs Weinstein can not even talk to her friends about him without becoming teary, and saying how lamentable he is. In any case, you're an engaged man.'

'I only want a game of tennis. She seems so alone.'

'Why don't you ask one of the girls to take her out to lunch?'

There was a long pause. Gladys was about to leave the table.

'Where is her husband?' said Michael, not even glancing up from his plate.

'Husband? Nobody knows if Ruth is even married. I can't help you any further. If you want her number, it's in the book on the hall table.' She paused and spoke as if she were thinking aloud. 'She must have been quite young when she had her child. She's still in her twenties.'

Ruth had sounded surprised and hesitant when she heard the invitation. She would like to play, but could her son come too? She hoped it would not be a nuisance, but the nanny had the day off.

Soon mother and son were standing in the hallway. Michael came down the dark-panelled staircase, and he could not help smiling when he saw her. He paused momentarily on the stair to relish the sight of her, here, in his own house. In the somber hallway, her white tennis outfit contrasted starkly with her dark hair.

Michael was so happy to see Ruth that it took a few moments to notice her son, who looked smaller than his eight years, and who hunched himself up close to his mother as if to make himself invisible. He was clutching her hand, and looking straight at him, with the unabashed look of childish curiosity. Two skinny legs protruded from a baggy pair of gray flannel shorts, and he leaned his weight on one side of his foot in nervousness. His eyes were wide and held a trace of sadness. Michael ignored his shyness and spoke loudly.

'Hello Ruth. Hello, young man. What's your name?'

The boy squirmed. His answer was barely audible. 'Ben, sir!'

Michael shook the small boy's hand warmly, hoping to loosen that melancholic expression. But the boy just looked down at his scuffed shoes, avoiding any further gaze.

'Mrs Waller will take care of you. I think she's got a surprise for you in the garden. Have you met Toby?'

A dog started yapping as if on cue from behind the kitchen door, and Mrs Waller emerged with a small snuffling terrier. Michael thought he saw her stop, almost imperceptibly, when she saw him and Ruth and smile to herself.

The boy could not contain his happiness. After looking for an assenting nod from his mother, he knelt down and tousled the dog's ears.

'That's a happy dog, now,' said Mrs Waller. 'He's going to need a feed, so follow me, young man!'

The compliant animal was scooped up by the boy, as it kicked its paws, frantically trying to find the ground.

'Come on Toby! Good boy! You come with me now' said the boy.

The morning sun was still cool, but its cloudless light reflected all the different greens of shrubs, bushes, and shimmering leaves. The neatly-mown lawn, still damp with dew, put a spring in the step of the two figures in their bright tennis whites. Michael felt he was in an aquarium, even the light seemed watery. He felt a strange contentment, a sybaritic drowsiness, as he walked beside Ruth. India was going to be a shock after an English summer.

The game was companionable. No need for small talk just the apology for a miss-hit and the welcome laughter after an impossibly retrieved ball. Ruth played with the same poise Michael had seen when he first saw her. Her movements were strong and graceful. Yet it was her laughter that was new. It came easily and spontaneously, and was in contrast to her recent gravity.

But such a casual bond was changing. Michael felt a seriousness looming over the couple like the gathering slate-grey clouds in the distant sky. He could not tell if it were good or bad. He only knew he had as little control over it as over the storm clouds that would soon bring warm rain for the plants.

They had just sat down on the lawn to drink Mrs Waller's lemonade when Michael saw a figure through the gap in the hedge, advancing quickly towards them. He felt a stab of guilt. It was Sarah, and she was frowning thunderously, though Michael could not tell whether she was angry or merely thoughtful. She was obviously on a mission. When she reached them she smiled and spoke to Michael.

'There you are. Your mother told me you were here. I brought some strawberries. I thought you might like some company, though I see you've found some already.'

Michael was embarrassed. Why did Sarah always make him feel guilty? He should have invited Sarah and another friend to play mixed doubles.

'Just an impromptu game,' he said. 'Sit down.'

His invitation was superfluous. Sarah had already sat down and she was looking at Ruth morosely.

'I'm sure your tennis is much better than mine' Ruth said to Sarah.

Sarah was forced into conversation. She asked her, 'Do you play much in Germany?'

'I used to. That's why I'm happy to play today. In Germany, in recent years, my mind has been on other things.'

'I can't believe tennis would be a problem there. Nothing more innocuous than tennis is there?' said Sarah. Her voice had a sarcastic edge, and Michael hoped Ruth did not notice it.

'Everything in Germany has changed. Everything,' said Ruth.

'I wouldn't allow myself to be intimidated and prevented from playing tennis. Good heavens!' Sarah was being too severe.

Michael's voice was gentle when he spoke.

'Are things really so bad in Germany?'

'They're worse than you can imagine. The humiliations...' Ruth stopped in mid-sentence.

'I always think humiliation is a state of mind, don't you think?' said Sarah.

Ruth ignored her comment, and continued. She told them how her father had his job at the university taken away from him. Jewish professors and civil servants were fired the previous year under Hitler's directions, she said. His powers were given to him under the Enabling Act, a law that 'enabled' him to become a tyrant. 'So,' she concluded, 'My father's funds are very low, now, and I worry about my parents, even their ability to go out and buy food without being harassed or attacked.'

'Is it possible to ride it out, to get a loan?' asked Michael.

'My father tried to obtain a loan from his bank,' said Ruth. 'The manager could not, or would not see him. A junior just turned his request down flat. Father said he was smirking as he did so and he repeated his refusal in front of everyone as they went into the Bank's lobby. His words were, 'I'm sorry, we do not lend to Jews'. My poor father!'

'But you get those sort of people here,' said Sarah. 'There's that man at the local bank, Bovis. I went in there the other day and he summoned me into his office like a school girl. I let him know how bad his manners were. You get prejudiced people everywhere, don't you, darling?' she asked Michael. It was the first time she had called him 'darling' and it made him uncomfortable.

Sarah was being purposefully obtuse. He wanted to support Ruth not Sarah. 'It's not just a question of prejudice Sarah', was all he managed to say, and he knew it sounded weak.

Ruth was exasperated. 'You don't understand. It's everywhere. It's against the Jews. I am Jewish. Imagine you are going past your local shops. Some have the Star of David painted on the windows. Only the shops owned by Jews. They tell you not to buy from the Jews, because that helps destroy the German economy. And what do you think would happen to the shop keepers if they tried to destroy the notices?'

'Everyone can ignore that behaviour. "Sticks and stones will break my bones but names will never hurt me",' said Sarah.

'They have sticks and stones. And broken bottles. And knives. Bones are broken,' said Ruth. She was reddening.

Michael wanted to change the subject. He could see Ruth was upset, but just as he was about to speak, Ruth continued.

'I have to tell you. I have to tell everyone. People here just do not understand what goes on there. A friend of my father's was put in the concentration camp. An innocent man, well-respected in the community. When he came back he had terrible panic attacks. He used to be elegant, but he became all disheveled. Then they found his diary. Just a diary! Do you keep a diary?' She looked at them. 'I do! He was taken away and no one has heard of him since.'

Sarah spoke out. 'I'm sure bad things happen. Injustices are everywhere. People were hanged here not long ago for stealing a sheep and ...'

Michael wanted to interrupt Sarah and explain that this was Germany, the land that produced Beethoven, Schopenhauer, and Goethe. In a supposedly civilized democracy, thugs were attacking people just because they were Jewish. Before he could say anything Ruth shot back at Sarah.

'It's not just the Jews, A very good friend of mine was targeted. A fellow student. I studied medicine with him until I was barred from classes because I was Jewish. This chap must have seemed the perfect type for the Nazis. Blond, blue-eyed and with a fine athletic physique.'

Michael felt uncomfortable. He wondered if Ruth was talking about Ben's father. He felt a jealousy that was out of place. Yet it was the nature of all men to feel possessive about a pretty woman, he thought.

'The trouble was that this man was known to be a communist,' said Ruth.

Sarah mumbled, 'I'm not too fond of communists myself,' but Ruth did not seem to hear her.

She continued, and her voice was urgent.

'His garden was dug up because they thought he had a machine gun. He did not even know what such a weapon looked like. They beat him anyway, to force a confession.' She stopped talking suddenly and picked roughly at some blades of grass. Her eyes were moist. Her two companions waited for her to continue. Her voice trembled. 'His body had boot marks all over the stomach, and there were fist-sized marks on the back. The post mortem said it was dysentery that sometimes causes death spots.'

Ruth looked up at Sarah. Her voice was again firm, but not angry, as she spoke to her.

'That's what's happening, Sarah. Happening all over Germany. Don't make light of it. Please.'

Sarah seemed to sneer as she spoke. 'Ruth, let's try not to get too emotional about it.'

This time Ruth was angry. 'Emotional? The lives of countless people are in danger, my parents included. It's not just their jobs, or their quality of life. It's their lives. Don't you understand? How can I make people like you see?'

Ruth had tears in her eyes by now. She stood up abruptly. Michael wanted to put his arm around her as he saw her struggling to hold back her tears, but he only managed to put his hand on her arm to console her, and utter inadequate words. 'I'm so sorry, Ruth' he said.

Ruth would not listen. She started half running toward the house. Michael was going to follow her, but he thought she would be embarrassed. She would want her privacy.

'My goodness! She gets upset easily,' Sarah exclaimed.

Michael could not hide his irritation.

'I think you under-estimate what she has been through'.

'Being a single mother can not help,' replied Sarah. 'It must make you a prey to all sorts of difficulties. And what sort of future does she have? No man is going to be interested in her, poor thing.'

MICHAEL SENSED THAT HIS MOTHER was plotting something. Estelle was coming to dinner and Gladys said they all needed to talk. 'Talk' was a sinister word because there was never a shortage of conversation when the two sisters got together. It was obvious to Michael that his mother wanted to confront him with some news.

Though a soldier, Michael always tried to avoid a certain type of conflict – emotional conflict. As a young boy, he had been doted on by his mother, and he felt that the world revolved around him. Boarding school had suddenly shattered his self-confidence. He had suffered terrible bullying at school. He had been small for his age until he was fifteen when there was a sudden spurt to his growth and, as an only child, he had not learned to defend himself against other children. The boys at school called him shrimp. At first it had seemed almost affectionate, but then it turned ugly. 'And what rhymes with shrimp?' they would say. 'Chimp!' Then they would all laugh and hoot, making chimp noises and scratching under their armpits. They shoved and pushed him in the corridors, making him drop his books. They tripped him up so that he would scrape his knee. They hid his uniform – his tie or one shoe – and when he started to look for them frantically, they would chant, 'Monkey looks for monkey nuts! Monkey looks for monkey nuts!'

He got into such trouble for losing things that he was caned by the masters. He remembered waiting, alone, outside the study for his punishment, while passing boys whispered and laughed at him. He remembered bending over the chair as he waited for the stinging thwack of the cane on the tops of his legs. Tears came to his eyes with the pain, tears he forced himself to suppress to avoid further taunts as he hobbled out of the master's study. Although sunny and extrovert by nature, he became outwardly shy and tentative. He learned that you had to fit in with the crowd to avoid pain and humiliation. Inwardly he felt his mother had abandoned him, and he developed an increasing disrespect for authority, even as outwardly he was careful to obey the rules and to be a 'good boy'. He felt the same reflex whenever he faced any disagreement whether it was with his mother, with his fellow officers or with the community. He would go with the crowd, or pretend to do so.

Tonight he was not in the mood for facing his mother's opprobrium, but he could tell there was no stopping her. He tried to look on the meal as a scene from one of his mother's plays, a contemporary farce, in which he was merely an actor. His aunt certainly added to the theatre of the situation, he thought, with her ability to subtly tease her sister and stir up her emotions. Yet he was wary about the pressures his mother could exert on him, and about the way she would stubbornly pursue him until she felt she had achieved her goal.

The meal did not start well. The sisters quarreled as soon as Mrs Waller brought in the casserole of Irish stew. She served slowly and Michael knew she was listening.

'Dora Cunningham is very upset at the moment. Her son has just made an outrageously bad match,' said Gladys.

'To that Australian girl?' asked Estelle.

'Yes, and it's affecting her role in the play.'

'What is she playing this time?' asked Michael. He knew that the business of the amateur dramatics club was not the real agenda of the evening, but he could only wait patiently for his mother to reveal the purpose of the meal.

'She's Lady Bracknell. You know, *The Importance of Being Earnest*. But she said to me, 'Gladys, I'm just not up to it tonight''

'She never was up to it,' said Estelle. 'It would be like Mrs Waller playing Lady Macbeth, don't you agree Mrs Waller?' Mrs Waller feigned distraction, as if she were not listening intently to the conversation but her unnatural, slow way of ladling the stew revealed her true preoccupation. 'What's that, Ma'am?' she asked, before she bustled back into the kitchen.

'Let's face it Gladys,' continued Estelle, you never could get casting right. What about that awful man who played Caesar? No decorum in the forum!'

'Not amusing, Estelle. I'm a very good caster. You only have to look at her to see she's Lady Bracknell,' said Gladys. 'Anyway, I was talking about her son's fiancée.'

Michael was impatient. He wished his mother would just cut to the chase and say what was on her mind. He could guess what it was. He sat there like a chess player, waiting for the predicted moves.

'She's not that much of a disaster,' said Estelle. 'I met the girl and she seemed a good sort. It's just stupid prejudices against a foreigner, like the prejudices surrounding that beautiful young lady, Ruth. Aren't I right, Michael?'

Michael ignored the question, but he could feel two sets of eyes fix on him, piercingly. He always suspected his aunt of scrutinizing him and using innocent questions to root out information. To his relief she left the question unanswered and continued. 'Admittedly the fiancée's proportions are as generous as our Lady Bracknell's, but I think young Cunningham will be happy with her.'

Gladys pursed her lips and looked disapproving. Estelle was thwarting the purpose of her meal in some way.

'You just don't understand, do you, Estelle? I know Dora has been cruel in her descriptions of the girl. She went quite overboard at the rehearsal when she called her old, fat and part aborigine. All untrue. But you're missing the point, as usual.' Gladys sighed and glanced significantly at Michael. 'It's her background'.

'What has background got to do with it?' asked Michael. He knew exactly what his mother was driving at now. It was her disapproval of his friendship with Ruth. He felt defiant, even though he knew his mother had nothing to worry about.

Both women looked at him as if he had just wiped his mouth with the back of his sleeve, as he used to do when he was small.

'John Cunningham comes from a very good family and it's a family you marry, not an individual,' said Gladys, wearily, as if she had repeated this like a mantra and it had still not sunk in.

'This is 1934, mother. We're not in the age of Jane Austen anymore,' said Michael.

'You worry me, Michael' said Gladys.

Estelle leaned across the table in a conspiratorial way, as if someone was lurking in the room to pick up her gossip. She appeared to relish her role as informer, pausing for effect before she spoke.

'The girl's father is rumored to be very wealthy. He owns a newspaper in Sydney, apparently'.

'Wealthy? What has wealth got to do with it? Money has never cut ice in England. It's class that counts' said Gladys.

'Rubbish, mother,' said Michael. 'Where do you think the English noble families came from? The king gave them titles to go with their wealth. He wanted to keep them sweet. Some of the oldest families in England made their money as sheep farmers. Now there's a lesson there, somewhere, for the Australians!'

Gladys now had the haughtiness of a school teacher. 'You've absorbed some very foolish ideas, Michael,' she said.' I suppose they're fashionable but I find it very disappointing that you can repeat them. You of all people! An army officer who has promised obedience to king and country. A place for each man and each man in his place. Every Englishman knows that!'

'You'll be advocating the Indian-style caste system next, mother. One of the biggest problems in India. And they don't even have to swear allegiance to king and country' said Michael.

'Rubbish, Michael. I'm talking about England.'

Michael was impatient. 'I can't believe you're saying this mother. Your own father was a shopkeeper.'

Gladys reddened, but Michael continued.

'I know he owned a chain of successful shops, but he was a tradesman, a shopkeeper nonetheless. Let's face it!'

Estelle tried to intervene. 'Michael, dear. That's disrespectful!'

'It's not aunt! Social mobility has made this country, just as it's made America great. We stopped believing in the divine right of kings and nobles when we chopped off the king's head back in 1649.'

'How did we arrive at this conversation?' said Gladys, looking at the ceiling in exasperation.

'He's right,' said Estelle. 'Terence's family wasn't out of the top drawer, but we couldn't have been happier and it would have been our thirtieth anniversary next month and though we didn't have children...'

Gladys was angry, and she became cruel. 'Be quiet! You and your rudderless diatribes, Estelle!' she said.

There was silence and Michael saw that Gladys was preparing to get to the point she had wanted to make all evening. 'Have you seen Peter lately?' she asked, a little too sweetly.

'Yes. You know I saw him at the garden party.'

'He's getting on very well with Vera. Such a sweet girl. Quite the trend-setter. Do you think it's a good match?'

Michael was ahead of his mother. He saw she was trying to speed up his wedding plans and dead-panned the conversation.

'More potatoes, aunt?'

Gladys was not to be stopped. She holds on to an idea like a bulldog locks on to the throat of his victim, thought Michael.

'You know, you could do a lot worse than Sarah. In fact she's a super girl. I was talking to her mother...'

'Not Cynthia Traverse' interrupted Estelle. 'You can't get a word in edgeways with her and she was such a disaster in the dramatics society she had to be sidelined to a flower arranging roster where...'

Gladys raised her voice and banged the table with her fist.. 'Enough, Estelle!' She paused and looked at Michael. 'The Traverse family has some exciting news for you, Michael. They won't mind if I tell you now.'

Michael looked up from his plate. He was always alarmed by his mother's 'exciting news'. He remembered when she told him he was going to boarding school. 'We've exciting news for you,' his mother had said. He had known what she was going to say. He had already been warned by older boys about his certain future. The bullying, the hard mattresses, and cold dormitories. He had felt bereft when, at the age of seven, she had left him at the school. So much for 'exciting news', he had thought. He had never heard such a sad sound as the gravel crunching under her departing car, as he watched her and she gave him no wave nor second glance. He had been so close to his mother up until that time, but from that moment of abandonment, a certain bond between them had been broken forever. His mother was not going to fool him now.

'What news?' he asked.

'Sarah and Vera are coming to India.'

Michael could not hide the relief in his voice.

'To India? It's a big place, mother. I doubt they'll be near me.'

'That's just the point, Michael. They will be staying for part of the time at your hill station, in Bakloh. Vera's parents know the colonel's wife so they'll be in her bungalow. It's all been arranged.'

Michael stopped chewing. He understood in a moment. He would be forced into a situation where Sarah and he would be considered partners by all the officers. He was already engaged but this would precipitate their union in everyone's eyes. Sarah would do everything to encourage that assumption. It seemed to him to be a plot, hatched by his mother and the Traverse family. He would have to entertain Sarah and Vera with picnics and tennis games. It would take all his efforts to steer a course between enthusiasm and indifference. Everyone he knew, even thousands of miles away, back in Camberley, would consider them married before the event. He now understood the purpose of the evening dinner, and the conversation about suitable marriages. He was at least glad that Estelle had not played the role his mother had planned for her that evening. Gladys was a bad caster after all. His aunt had not championed Sarah in the way Gladys wanted her to do.

There was a brief silence. Michael did not trust himself to talk with composure. He was going over his options in his mind. Maybe he shouldn't return to India at all. But he had to go back, He had made a promise to John. And this was one promise he was not about to break.

'They will be going on to Srinigar, where Peter thought you and he could join them,' continued Gladys.

'So Peter's in on this,' said Michael, through his teeth.

'Where is Srinigar?' asked Estelle.

Michael was glad of the distraction. He did not want his mother to know the full extent of his antipathy to the Indian travel plans.

'It's a resort in Kashmir, away from the heat and sweat of the rest of India. There's a beautiful lake where people, mostly army wives, have houseboats. It would be peaceful, but for all the partying and intrigues. Luckily most husbands are in blissful ignorance of their wives' behaviour, while they are toiling away back in the sweaty plains The place reminds me of the revolving bedroom doors of the old French court.'

'Oh how shocking!' said Estelle, smiling and not looking in the least bit perturbed.

'Michael doesn't need to mix with that sort,' said Gladys. 'Apart from anything else, he has his career to think about, don't you Michael?'

Michael grinned at his aunt.

'I am the very paragon of discretion', said Michael.

'I have a word of advice, paragon!' said Gladys.

Advice was another word of his mother's to which Michael had an aversion. He recalled her advice that he should not go to university, but should train for the army at Sandhurst. The advice was really a command. It was made clear there would be no moral or financial support for his dreams of academe.

'I know Estelle supports me on this one. You should not socialize with Ruth.'

'I'm not a child, for heaven's sakes, mother,' said Michael.

'Nonetheless, I'm your mother and I tell you it's not right. You're engaged. People are already talking about the attention you paid her at the garden party. You would never fit in with this community if you pursued her and it would ruin your career. It would be a disaster.'

Michael wanted to ignore his mother but he could not refrain from challenging her. 'What do you mean disaster? What's wrong with Ruth?' he asked.

'I don't have to spell it out. You could not stay in the army with a wife who had a past. A child. Then there is her religion. You really are obtuse sometimes!'

'Mother, please trust me with my own decisions!'

Gladys stood up.

'I've said what I needed to stay. Now it's late. At least I've warned you, Michael.'

She looked piqued as she turned and left the room. Michael and Estelle were left looking at each other.

'Time for the port, dear,' said Estelle. 'And no half measures for me!'

CHAPTER 7

SARAH IN INDIA! Michael felt uncomfortable with the idea. He did not know why. He could not understand why the message had to come from his mother. He had to talk to Sarah. She would have to reassure him that the visit would merely be a pleasant interlude; that there would be no pressure to advance the wedding plans.

Early next morning, Michael telephoned Sarah to arrange a meeting. He knew that she would be at home, because she worked as her father's secretary on most weekday mornings.

The entrance to the colonel's house was meant to be imposing. A wide driveway led up to the mock Tudor house, with its leaded windows and half-timbered gables. The shrubs, standing sentinel either side of the front door, were trimmed into neat symmetric cones.

The door was answered by Traverse himself, who impatiently waved aside a uniformed maid, as if she had been too slow in answering the bell. Michael was shocked by his appearance. He was not in his black shirt but his outfit was just as startling. He wore baggy plus fours in a loud Prince of Wales check. He was the parody of a country squire. His eyes were even more distracting than his attire. His right eye sported a large monocle which distorted it and unnaturally widened the lids. The eyeball seemed to be enlarged further by the refraction of the glass, so it glared back at him, fish-like.

'Michael, my boy! Come in!'

Michael followed this ersatz rural gent into the drawing room. He knew the house well, ever since he had been a Sandhurst cadet, taking Sarah out to dances and to the pictures with their friends. The drawing room had not changed except for one glaring detail. There were still the silver-framed photographs on every surface, depicting the colonel in uniform meeting a variety of dignitaries. The heavy late-Victorian furniture crowded the room as it had always done, and the mahogany framed sofa sat like a booby trap for the uninitiated. People would let themselves sink into to its velvet upholstery, only to discover a bumpy landing and impossibly uncomfortable seat that distracted them from any cogent conversation. Funereal dark wooden plinths, topped with aspidistra plants, were placed strategically in the same positions around the room ready to overbalance at the slightest misstep of the inalert and large urn-like vases holding dried hydrangeas staked out precious space, marginalizing guests to the strict seating arrangement. Everything, then, was the same except for the one new feature in the room, that stood out so starkly it was intimidating. It was an enormous oil painting of the colonel himself, in khaki uniform, with a string of medals on his chest. It had pride of place, and hung on the wall over the fireplace which was piled high with unseasonal logs.

The colonel saw Michael look at the portrait.

'Damn good artist, wouldn't you say? He's shown at the Royal Academy.'

Michael nodded, unable to go so far as to praise the work, although the colonel paused expectantly, waiting for the compliment. He sounded curt when it did not come.

'So you've come to see Sarah, have you? Takes me back to the days when I courted the little woman.'

Try as he might, Michael could not picture Mrs Traverse, doyenne of so many of Camberley's 'ladies' committees', as the little woman. It was true she showed devotion and loyalty to her husband whenever possible, praising his intelligence and getting people to agree on his great achievements. But she, like her husband, was not a humble, behind-the-scenes type.

'Her parents were only too pleased to see me', continued the colonel. 'Thought she was going to be left on the shelf. Practically begged me to take her off their hands! Ha! Ha!'

It was difficult to smile convincingly, so Michael smirked, and then felt afraid it could be taken as mockery. But the colonel did not notice, and did not even stop to draw breath.

'Of course Sarah has many admirers.' The colonel wagged his finger in Michael's face. 'You're a lucky fellow, Michael.'

Michael again tried to smile and remained silent. He was hoping for a pre-prandial drink, even though it had only just turned midday. He eyed some crystal decanters with amber liquid sitting on a shelf in a far corner of the room through some aspidistra leaves, but there was no offer of refreshment, not even tea.

The door opened and Sarah strode in.

'Ah, Michael! There you are!' He felt like a tardy schoolboy.

Sarah was wearing a dress of the same floral pattern that Ruth had worn at the Garden Party. Michael wondered if her choice was intentional. 'Probably just a coincidence,' he thought. It was not well-tailored and looked lumpy on her, and a bow at the collar made her look like a badly-wrapped gift, thought Michael.

The colonel looked at Sarah and then at Michael with a proprietorial sense of pride.

'I'll just leave you two then, while I sort out some business. My time is so taken up these days. Still, someone has to show the way!'

Michael waited for the door to click shut before getting straight to the point.

'Sarah, my mother told me that you and Vera are coming to India.'

'Yes!' said Sarah. 'What a hoot! It was meant to be a surprise, and I couldn't wait to see your face when I told you. But nothing can be kept under wraps for long in Camberley, can it?'

'I just wish you had planned it with me instead of springing it on me,' said Michael

'Springing it on you! Really, Michael! I was planning to tell you today, but your mother must have got wind of it. Anyone would think you were less than delighted. Still, you're such a plodder when it comes to planning things. I just hope the wedding plans won't be done at your usual tortoise pace.'

'I'm talking about India, Sarah! I feel it was not right to leave me in the dark about it.'

'Don't be silly. I couldn't tell you before I was sure. Just relax and enjoy the prospect of having me there.'

'And Vera!' added Michael.

'Yes, and Vera.' Her voice took on an accusing edge. 'Peter is really keen to see her over there.' The barb had been felt and she lightened her tone. 'Come on! Buck up! It's going to be such fun. A good preparation for when I come out permanently.'

'I . . . I just don't know that's it's a good idea,' said Michael hesitantly.

Sarah was combative. 'You still love me, don't you?

'I would not be engaged to you if I didn't feel for you,' he replied.

'Well this is a chance to show how much you do love me.' We'll all have a real hoot, you'll see. She paused momentarily. 'I have a little surprise for you.'

Michael waited.

'There's a performance in the West End of that new Noel Coward play, *Conversation Piece.* I was given tickets and would like you to come with me tonight? It's short notice, but the tickets are gifts.'

Michael hesitated, but could think of no good reason to avoid the outing.

Sarah took his hesitation as assent.

'It's at His Majesty's Theatre, with that French actress, Yvonne Printemps. We'll set off after tea.'

They drove toward London in the bright afternoon. Michael felt lighthearted. He could not be angry with Sarah for long. Her buoyancy was contagious. She regaled him with gossip and their laughter united them.

The theatre was just by Leicester Square, in the busy street of Haymarket. It was an imposing building, built like a French Chateau, with a central gray-domed roof, an imposing stone facade with tall windows and central colonnades. The setting was appropriate, since the heroine of the play was a young woman fleeing the French Reign of Terror.

The crowd pressed into the theatre lobby in their finery, talking excitedly, the women in long clinging dresses and arm length white gloves. In spite of the summer warmth, they swaddled themselves in fur and silk stoles. The men wore top hats and white ties, their fringed white silk scarves dangling loosely over their shoulders. Sarah wore a blue satin dress, cut on the bias, and would have been elegant but for an affected diamante tiara resting on her curls and clumpy shoes that made her waddle rather than glide.

It was only after the play that Michael's mood changed, unexpectedly. Up until that time, he thought he had enjoyed the play, with its artful clichés of Regency rakes, its impoverished, noble heroine, in pursuit of love. He had laughed at Coward's witty dialogue, especially when Madame Printemps had asked her consort, in an appalling French accent 'When may I lurve somebody'. 'Not until you are safely married, and zen only with ze greatest discretion', he replied, adding, 'Emotion is so very untidy.' It was all so British, yet when he came into the cool evening air something about the play made Michael increasingly uncomfortable. Sarah did not share his feeling. She hummed one of the jauntier numbers as she walked and it seemed to put a bounce in her step in spite of the shoes. The puzzle, thought Michael, was that he disliked the jocularity. It was a mask for something sinister. Then he realized why he felt disturbed. The Regency era was not just about Beau Brummell, Prince George and the Brighton Pavilion. It was about violence and tyranny threatening to engulf Europe. It was about bloodshed and battlefields. Yet for those regency rakes, the dance went on, in the bright London theatres and ballrooms, just as it did now.

The couple had decided to walk through the streets to the restaurant at the Savoy. They walked across Trafalgar Square with its massive lion statues, the maned heads raised in watchfulness, and the towering monument to Nelson that seemed to be a lookout. The memorial only plunged Michael deeper into his unwelcome thoughts of encroaching danger across the Channel. He was not even allowed to forget India. There, by one of the swishing fountains, was the upright statue of a Victorian man, a hero of the Indian mutiny. Major General Sir Henry Havelock. He was planted on his plinth, forever imperturbable in his frock coat, assailed only by pigeons, now a sanitized version of history in spite of the bird droppings. Unlike the crowds that passed by the statue daily, Michael knew what the hero had seen. The killing fields, the horror of battle, yet there he was, set in cool bronze. It made Michael want Sarah to distract him with her prattle, but they were walking too fast and the streets were noisy. There was a constant hubbub around them of snatched conversations, motor engines, and car horns. Their footsteps echoed on the pavements as they pushed through groups of theater-goers trying to hire cabs and knots of people in drabber clothes pressing into pub doorways. Darkness was finally falling and the stars were clear against the night sky, in spite of the competing lights of the cars, the interior lights of half-empty double Decker buses, bright restaurant doorways and street lamps.

They were nearing the six storied façade of Charing Cross station, which Michael always felt looked more like a huge French *Mairie* than a railway terminus. The crowds were getting thicker and Michael noticed a couple of swaying drunks in shabby jackets, clutching bottles. The area took on a menacing air. He was reminded of a friend who had been pick-pocketed and badly beaten by some thugs near the station a few months earlier. They passed a darkened alley and Sarah suddenly shrieked. Michael saw an arm in a grimy tweed sleeve stick out at knee level barring their way. It was clutching a tin cup. The crumpled figure of a down-and-out could be seen behind the arm, in the gloom. An incoherent voice came from the shadows.

'Oh my!' said Sarah. 'Get him away! Get him away!'

Michael saw the man had only one arm. In his mind's eye he suddenly saw one of the soldiers in his regiment who had to have his arm amputated after being injured by a booby-trap. He couldn't pass this man by. He gently maneuvered himself between the tramp and Sarah.

'It's all right, Sarah! He only wants some change.'

He pulled some loose change from his pockets and threw it clattering into the cup. The arm shot back into obscurity.

The couple walked on. Sarah shuddered with relief.

'You'll have to get used to beggars in India, Sarah!' said Michael.

'Why can't the police do their job and get rid of that scum?' she asked.

'Many of those beggars are desperate, they have nothing to eat and nowhere to live. Some are disabled soldiers' said Michael.

'It's so disgusting. Britain ought to clean up its streets. They ought to put people like that away.'

Of all the differences between them, Sarah's lack of compassion for people living on the streets was the one that he had the most trouble overlooking. Perhaps Sarah was too sheltered from the rougher sides of life to understand reasons for men's misery. Or perhaps she felt too insecure to allow herself to imagine herself in a similar situation. Michael empathized. He could not stop himself. Instinctively he knew that somewhere inside he was injured, just like this man. Sarah did not know this side of Michael.

'We won't allow that to spoil our evening,' he said.

The bonhomie was restored by the short walk to the Strand and they were soon being seated at a linen-clothed table in the restaurant. They had a view of the river, which glistened darkly beneath them, and reflected the lights from the banks. Inside, the muted light of the chandelier and candles revealed groups of elegant diners of all ages. A band played a soft, wistful melody, a Noel Coward song, and Michael recalled the lyrics:

> A room with a view
> And you
> And no one to worry us
> No one to hurry us
> Through this dream we've found.

A few couples swayed on the dance floor and Michael felt light-headed and sentimental. He attributed it to the effects of the first sips of champagne that the waiters had presented to them so quickly from the napkin-swathed bottle.

Sarah suddenly broke his thoughts by speaking in a clipped, precise tone, as if she had prepared a speech.

'Michael, I don't want you seeing that woman Ruth.'

'What do you mean, Sarah? She's only a neighbour.'

'She's a Harpy. You're just the sort of man who could fall into her clutches.'

Michael laughed.

'I'm serious Michael. Don't underestimate her. She's very bossy. Conniving.'

'Sarah, I'm just being friendly. I almost feel that she's a fellow soldier. The things she must have seen in Germany are unimaginable.'

'Lord, but you're gloomy sometimes, Michael. All I'm saying is stay away from women like Ruth. I don't know why you have to make a song and dance about it.'

Michael smiled and reached across the table to touch her hand.

'Talk about dancing, allow me!'

Michael was a good dancer and guided Sarah expertly around the dance floor, making her ill-chosen shoes seem light. But the sentimental words kept echoing in his head.

> And sorrows will never come.
> O will it ever come true,
> A room with a view?

Sarah's exhortations had had exactly the opposite effect to what was intended. He had been confronted by the image of Ruth and it was as if she were in the room with him, looking at him, her dark eyes reading his thoughts. Somehow he knew that Ruth was a fellow-traveller, someone who, like him had battle-scars that you couldn't see, and it drew him to her.

CHAPTER 8

MICHAEL HAD A DIFFICULT DUTY to perform before he went back to India. He had enlisted the help of Macleod to ease the burden and he was on his way to pick him up.

The gravel crunched and popped under the tyres. It was raining heavily and the windscreen wipers were tapping out a crazed rhythm.

Just as he stopped in front of the door, it was flung open and through the misty window of the car Michael saw an emerging figure. The face was obscured as a large black umbrella opened, but Michael recognized the elegant stockinged legs and high-heeled shoes. He opened the door, oblivious of the rain. He felt a burst of excitement.

'Ruth! Can I give you a lift?'

The umbrella was raised upright to reveal a startled expression.

'Michael! No. Thank you. I'll be fine. '

There was no smile. Michael wondered what Ruth could be doing at Macleod's house.

'Please!' said Michael. 'I'm driving Reverend Macleod to a meeting. I really don't think you should be out in this weather.'

Ruth was angry. Her words poured out. 'You weren't so concerned about me the last time we met. I thought your profession is to defend but you didn't help me when I was under attack from Sarah. Why are you so half-hearted when it comes to standing up for people? And don't tell me it's just British reserve.'

Michael put his hand quickly on her arm. 'I thought I did defend you. When you were upset I thought you needed to be by yourself or I would have followed you. Please. Get in the car.'

By now the brim of his hat was spilling water on to his raincoat and his face was moist. There was silence but for the sound of raindrops on the taut umbrella and the distant gushing of gutters.

Suddenly the door opened again and the dark figure of Macleod, approached them, hunched against the rain, with the collar of his raincoat turned up.

'Quickly, let's go, 'he said. 'You've no car, Ruth? Hop in. We'll take you home.'

Ruth could not refuse and sat in the passenger seat, staring ahead of her.

Macleod climbed into the back seat, squeezing his tall frame through the door with difficulty. He clapped his hands together and rubbed away the damp chill of the rain. 'Just the sort of weather for the pub.' He said. 'Shame we can't all go there now. "There's nothing worth the wear of winning, but laughter and the love of friends." Now who said that? Somebody with the right priorities. '

'It's good to see you again, Ruth,' said Michael. He paused, hoping she would explain why she was with Macleod, but she remained silent. He felt a curious jealousy that he quickly dismissed as irrational.

'Ruth was telling me about your tennis game,' said Macleod, speaking too loudly from the back seat in order to be heard above the rain and the noise of the car.

'I only said it was fun to have a chance to play again,' said Ruth.

'Michael can spot a good player when he sees one. It's not every one who's asked to play, is it Michael? 'For many are called, but few are chosen'.'

'No', said Michael. 'I'm very choosy about my partners.'

He looked at Ruth and smiled. He noticed she too smiled, though she was trying to hide her face as she looked down at her lap, adjusting her raincoat.

'I'm teaching Ben', said Ruth. 'I have a new game. It's a ball on elastic that you hit with a racket'.

'Ben's been feeling a bit lonely lately, hasn't he Ruth?' said Macleod. 'He could do with some male company. Perhaps you could help out, Michael?'

'I'd like that', said Michael. He could not understand why Macleod was trying to encourage his friendship with Ruth. After all, he would not consider her a suitable partner for him and he knew of his engagement to Sarah. He had a fleeting suspicion that Macleod's banter was a ruse to camouflage the fact that Ruth was visiting him, unescorted. After all, it could not have been on parish business.

'Don't worry. Ben's doing fine. We're still getting used to England. That's all.'

'I would like to see him. Would it be all right to drop by sometime?'

Ruth turned her face away and looked through the rain-streaked window, brushing the condensation with her gloved hand.

Michael took her silence as affirmation. 'That's settled then. Perhaps this afternoon?'

'But it's raining,' said Ruth.

'I'm an optimist' said Michael. 'It'll clear up.'

'If it doesn't you can always teach Ben those card games I used to play with you when you were young,' said Macleod.

'Yes, and you were ruthless,' said Michael. 'You always won'.

'Only when we were playing for pennies,' said Macleod.

'You see, Ruth. A man of the Church who gambles and outsmarts his opponents!'

'I was doing you a favor, Michael. 'Lucky at cards, unlucky in love'. I wanted to make you lucky in love.'

There was silence in the car. Ruth sounded formal when she spoke. 'You can come to see Ben whenever you wish, Michael'

'Thank you Ruth. And it's not just him I'm coming to see.'

They had arrived at Mrs Weinstein's house and Ruth was about to get out.

'Wait a minute', said Michael. He got out of the car and ran around to open her door. They huddled together under the confined shelter of the umbrella. Michael took Ruth's arm.

'I'll see you soon, Ruth,' he said.

'Yes all right,' she answered. It was enough encouragement for him.

Michael and Macleod were soon sheltering in the porch of a spacious Edwardian villa, much like Michael's own home. No one was answering the bell. The rain was still beating down and Michael looked up at a low, wispy cloud, being blown under the metallic gray sky. Like a ghost, he thought.

It was not the rain that made him uncomfortable, though.

'I feel like I'm at the dentist's about to face the pliers' he told his companion.

Michael felt a natural intimacy with Macleod. It was almost as if he were talking to his father again, sharing his feelings.

'Don't worry. Just think of how you are helping. I always find that gets me through. Try to forget about yourself and put yourself in the position of the other person.'

A young woman in a maid's uniform opened the door tentatively, and after nodding silently, showed them through to a large ordered sitting room with French windows, ajar in spite of the rain. A curtain on one side of the glass was twitching in the breeze. Chintz-covered armchairs and a large sofa were arranged facing each in anticipation of a face to face conference. They remained standing uncomfortably.

'They'll be a few minutes yet', said the young woman.

Michael saw some silver framed photographs on the mantel. He pointed to one.

'That's him!'

It was a picture of a young boy, round faced and smiling. He wore a sailor suit and was sitting in the lap of a smiling man in army uniform.

Macleod looked at the photograph and breathed a deep sigh.

'He never did reach a decent age,' said Michael. 'Twenty seven, like me. Sometimes I think my mother is right and I should just pack it in. Find a job in advertising or something.'

'His death hit you hard,' said Macleod.

'I was there. I saw it all. He was my friend'

'How did it happen? His parents couldn't tell me the details.'

Michael was keen to discuss the day that went through his mind like a film every night while he tried to sleep. He had been near the Afghan border with a group of twenty four men. Twelve of them, including John Fairbrother, were stuck, unable to advance on a ridge, held by the enemy. They were at risk of being picked off by enemy fire from the rocks just ahead of them and, to avoid such an impasse, they had to retreat down the steep hillside, towards Michael and his men, who were waiting in the relative safety of a small gully. The tribesmen were firing from the summit. Michael and his men tried to keep the enemy back by machine-gunning the crest of the hill, and then, all of a sudden, the signal to run back down the mountain was flagged up to them, and they were off. They reacted like runners to a starting gun.

'So it didn't work?' asked Macleod. 'Were many lost?'

'It was working. Beautifully. They were coming down like the clappers. Dust and stones were everywhere. Then John caught his foot in a crevice. He was in terrible pain. You could see it on his face. The others were ahead of him and they were lucky. They managed to join us in the safety of the gully. We had no time to help John.'

'At least it was quick.'

Michael was not used to euphemisms.

'No. I wouldn't say he died quickly. I can't get that picture out of my mind.'

'What picture, Michael?'

'He had tried to drag himself forward. His face all twisted. Then he was shot. He was on his stomach with his arms stretching in front of him. I can still see his eyes.' Michael stared ahead of him as he re-lived the scene. 'Unnaturally wide. It looks as if he's trying to hold his breath. One hand stretches forward, as if to grab an unknown hand. It's beseeching me. Then I think, 'he's trying to say something'. I want to know what it is. It's probably the pain, though. His body starts to twitch, but it's all over. I know he's dead. It's that picture of him stretching his hand out towards me. It won't leave me.'

'It never does, Michael.'

Michael looked at Macleod, surprised by his answer. He had his head bowed, and his shoulders were slumped. He would not look back at Michael, and continued to stare at the floor.

'You know, then? You've been through something like this, haven't you?'

'I...I'll tell you another time. I understand what...'

At that moment the door opened. A gaunt middle-aged woman in a back dress sidled into the room without meeting their gaze. She was followed by a man of similar age walking, stiffly. His appearance was startling. He looked elegant enough in a light brown suit, with regimental tie, but he seemed crumpled. A corner of his collar stuck up almost comically. His hair had been combed hastily and a large strand was standing on end in imitation of the collar. It was the eyes that were most noticeable. They had no luster, just a red tinge. The lids were swollen and dark rings framed the orbits.

These were the bereaved parents, Colonel and Mrs Fairbrother, and Michael was there to give them some comfort. Yet his own agitation was increasing. He knew that talking to the Fairbrothers would force him to confront ideas that he was trying to keep at the back of his mind. Fear of his own death, doubts about his usefulness in India. What would he have left if he lost his faith in the Empire?

'No formalities please, gentlemen. So good of you to come,' said the colonel.

'You received my letter from Bakloh, sir?' asked Michael.

'Yes, we did. Thank you' whispered the old man.

''I wanted you both to know how greatly I …we all… miss John. He was the best.'

The colonel did not seem to be listening. He was turning a signet ring on his small finger. His wife suddenly straightened her back and fixed her eyes on Michael. The look was accusing

'Perhaps you can tell me, Michael, Reverend, what our son died for?' she said.

'Hush, not now, dear!' said her husband.

She was unrelenting.

'Because it wasn't for some worthless rocks in Afghanistan.'

'No,' said Michael. 'It was for England. For the security of India, for the Empire.'

'Empire! You know who are behind the Empire? Fat cats, businessmen, making their piles of money in safety, while young men die.'

'John was keeping India safe, and not just for the British,' said Macleod. 'He was helping people, as he always did. Even as a small boy. Do you remember? Our pensioners loved him. He was always running errands for them.' He beamed sunnily at the memory of the small, irrepressibly eager boy.

Mrs Fairbrother's expression changed. She looked forlorn.

'Remember? I remember everything. I remember him as a baby, smiling a toothless smile. I remember his first day at school, holding my hand so tightly it hurt. And our jokes. We were the oldy mouldies.'

Then she too smiled for the first time as she became absorbed by her memories and she looked younger. There was a glimpse of the elegant, vivacious woman she must once have been.

'It wasn't always easy. Every parent knows that. All the love and the worry.' She turned to her husband. 'You remember, James, when he had that fever as a tiny baby, or when he cut his knee open on that broken glass?'

They were both silent. Michael wanted to change the conversation. He could see Mrs Fairbrother was fighting back tears. Her mouth was trembling. Before he could speak, she began to talk again.

'And now what? In the end we couldn't save him, could we? We didn't protect him. It was our fault. My son. My precious son. If we didn't still have our daughter, I don't think I could go on'

She tried to stifle her sobs in her handkerchief, as her husband put his arm around her shoulders. Macleod leant forward in his chair, one hand on his brow, shielding his eyes. Michael wondered if he was praying.

Michael suddenly wanted to leave the room. He wanted to run away from the sadness. But he could not. The sadness was his own.

Macleod looked up at the stricken parents. For the first time Michael noticed the lines of age in Macleod's face. It was as if his appearance had changed since he had walked into the room. He looked gaunt. 'God is with you, just as He is with John,' said Macleod.

Michael looked carefully to see if the words comforted the Fairbrothers. They did not console him, so how could they console the parents? Where was God on the day of John's death? Whose side was He on when He was invoked by both sides? Macleod said that the Pathan were fervent believers in the one God. Michael too believed in the one God.

But how could the God they knew be the one that he knew? They were ruthless barbarians. He could not believe in God's mercy for them.

The couple seemed calmer.

'I'm sorry. It's so difficult for us at the moment. You arranged such a wonderful memorial service. He really did lay his life down for others, didn't he? The "greater love" of the bible you spoke about,' said Mrs Fairbrother.

Macleod nodded. He then produced a large handkerchief from his pocket, and blew his nose noisily.

'And I'm sorry that Colonel Traverse gave you such a hard time,' said Colonel Fairbrother. ' My wife put him right. I don't know if you know that. Sent him off with a flea in his ear.'

Michael did not know what the colonel was talking about and Macleod gave no reaction. He would ask Macleod later. He suddenly saw Mrs Fairbrother looking at him with an intensity he found disconcerting. He knew what she was going to ask him, and he had dreaded the question. He had wanted above all else to keep secret his main motivation for returning to India.

'There was a girl, wasn't there, Michael?'

He tried to sound breezy. 'A girl? O yes! There was a girl. I don't know how serious it was.'

'It was very serious" said Mrs Fairbrother, while her husband sat immobile, staring at the floor. 'So serious that we had an anonymous letter about it. And then a brief note from John saying that he would explain everything later.' She sounded angry again. 'Only there wasn't a later, was there?'

Michael remained silent, hoping the conversation would stop, but Mrs Fairbrother continued, relentlessly. Michael knew now where John had inherited his outspokenness.

'I want to know who the girl is. Please. It would help us, it might help her. Can't you see that?'

Michael had no choice but to give an explanation. He would be careful, though. He would give no hint of the girl's name, or her whereabouts. He would re-consider only when he had visited her in India, to fulfil a mission John had given him in case of his death.

Michael began the story that had brought with it such chaos. He had seen the romance grow unexpectedly, like a stray seed taking root in arid soil. It would have been heartening, a happy ending would have been wished for, but there was an insurmountable problem. The girl was Anglo-Indian.

She was attractive, even beautiful, and lived a comfortable, European-style life with her mother in the hill station and resort near Bakloh, called Dalhousie. The girl was called Jane and her mother was Mary. Michael did not tell the Fairbrothers that their surname was British, Parry. That could unmask them too easily.

Mary's origins were a mystery. She looked more Indian than European. It was rumored that her father had held a high position in the Indian civil service, and that she was illegitimate. 'Born on the wrong side of the sheets' as one junior officer had put it in the mess. The identity of the husband, 'Mr Parry', was as murky as that of her father. Yet Mary was accepted, begrudgingly, on the fringes of British society in Dalhousie. Her apparent affluence had eased her admission into the community and she hosted a number of small parties, filled with soldiers from different regiments, church people, and the less snobbish army families.

It was at one of these parties that Michael had met Mary. He had not taken much notice of her then. He had been far more interested in her daughter Jane. She was a beautiful girl with a delicate oval face and fine bone structure. She looked Italian rather than Eurasian, although her almond-shaped eyes had a hint of the orient. Michael could see why John Fairbrother had fallen in love with her. John's admiration for Jane had been returned, but their love affair had to be kept secret from all but Michael and Jane's mother. This was to protect them against the gossip and inevitable prejudice that surrounded a match between a man and woman from different factions. But the situation was a time bomb that could ruin both John and Jane.

Michael had felt indignant about this need for secrecy. He felt the British had no right to fulminate against the injustices of the Hindu caste system, when their own racial prejudices made people like John and Jane suffer needlessly.

Then disaster struck. The secret was discovered and John's persecution began. Michael became more outraged. He had to listen to officers in the mess gossiping about Mary and laughing at her pretensions. They were hypocrites in accepting her hospitality, just as some of his fellow countrymen were hypocrites in lining their pockets in India, while disrespecting Indians. Yet Michael felt powerless to help his friend, and he found it hard to bear.

The insults that John had to endure grew worse and Michael had wondered how it would end. John would have to dump the girl, though she would remain disgraced in the eyes of the Dalhousie European community. But the liaison could not endure. It was not that his fellow officers were deliberately cruel. Michael knew them too well to believe that. They simply did not understand the depths of John's attachment to Jane, and they perhaps thought that making light of the situation would help him. It was a credit to John that he did not lose his temper. Michael had watched him as officers in the mess laughed at Jane's mother, imitating her speech and saying that she would go to any lengths to marry her daughter to a British officer, 'even if he looked like a camel' said one, 'Or the backside of a camel' said another. 'Of course she doesn't have parties', the conversation continued. 'No, she has soirées!' 'Sari soirées.' John had sat quietly sipping his drink as the laughter echoed around him.

It had all seemed so simple when John had first met Jane. It was not just love that made him blind to the divisions felt by all the factions in India, the British, the Hindus, the Muslims, the Sikhs – divisions that even existed within their own subsets. John was incapable of snobbery. Fellow officers often accused him of being naive. He was popular among the ranks for his lack of pompousness and he was always being asked to play tennis with visiting Indian officers, who sensed his natural ease in their company. But it was not naivety, thought Michael. It was quite the opposite. John was too intelligent, too worldly to judge anyone by the lottery of their birth.

The scandal of John's relationship was spiraling out of control. John had to endure 'talks' with senior officers about the difficulties of such a liaison, and the danger it posed for his career. He was told that censure and gossip would affect Jane and her mother, and that his pursuit of Jane was selfish. It was a barb that hurt John most of all because many people had begun to snub Mary's social gatherings and had turned their backs on them at the little Anglican church near their home. Leaving Jane was put to him as an act of altruism, the one means of persuasion that was likely to sway John.

So Michael was John's confidant. John had told him of his plans to marry Jane, plans that had been formulated as soon as he had set eyes on her. He insisted that it was not just 'lust' at first sight. Jane seemed to be a shy young woman, but, said John, her reticence masked a sharp intelligence. She was well-read, though mainly self-taught. They had a lot in common.

Then there was a further complication. Soon after the first confidences, John had become anxious. When they were alone, sitting together on the verandah of the officer's mess, one peaceful evening, savouring the view of the mountains and the echo of birdsong, John had told Michael that they had consummated their relationship. Jane's mother was not watchful, and John suspected that she tacitly ignored their trysts, hoping it would lead to marriage. John was so honorable; Michael knew that John had reached the point of no return with Jane.

Soon the pressure was ratcheted up. Tongues had been wagging so fiendishly that the affair was brought to the colonel's attention. He had summoned John and warned him sternly about his alliance. But John had been defiant. It was clear his career and his reputation were about to be ruined. He had even stood up in the mess one night to challenge anyone who criticized him to do so to his face. Michael, who was sitting next to him, had admired his courage. Naturally, no one did confront him and there had only been smirks of embarrassment or, perhaps, amusement. No doubt many thought that John had had just a little too much to drink. The rumor was that the whole thing would blow over, that it was the infatuation of a healthy full-blooded male starved of female company.

But there were some who were not so indulgent. John was to suffer further betrayal when some one wrote anonymously to inform his parents about Jane. His parents had been sympathetic, according to John, and had simply urged him not to do anything rash and that they would talk about the situation when he returned to England on his forthcoming leave. They had not realised the extent of the crisis and the pressure John was under.

It was under this cloud of uncertainty and censure that John had gone into battle and was killed. Michael had wondered if the stress had affected his reactions and so, in an indirect way, led to his death.

This was the story, with tactful omissions, that Michael told to the Fairbrothers, as they sat still, Mrs Fairbrother leaning toward Michael, on the edge of the sofa.

'I was a witness to John's love for Jane', Michael concluded. 'It brought them both great happiness, for a time. That's all there is to tell.'

'No it isn't!' said Mrs Fairbrother. 'You still haven't told us how we can contact the girl,' she said. 'What has happened to her? Is she all right? Could we share our memories of John with her?'

Mrs Fairbrother seemed to think the girl's origins were irrelevant. That, and her defiance of the commonly held views, reminded Michael of John.

Michael was non-committal. He was anxious to hide his connection to Jane. He could let nothing, not even John's parents, sabotage the meeting he had planned with Jane on his return to India. He felt himself being scrutinised and was nervous lest any facial expression would expose his secretiveness. 'I will make enquiries,' he said. 'Yes,' said Mrs Fairbrother. ' I hope you will do so. You can do it from here, in Camberley, couldn't you?' 'I will do my best, Mrs Fairbrother,' said Michael, adding hurriedly, 'We'd better go now and leave you in peace'.

'Go?' said Mrs Fairbrother, as if responding to a cue.

'Your going back to India soon, aren't you, Michael?' she continued. 'It's none of my business, but I'll say it anyway. I don't think you should go. You are in danger. I have a strange feeling about your service there.'

Michael was taken aback. He knew that grief accounted for her words, but they were eerie. They were the words of an oracle, warning him.

'We believe in premonition' said the colonel. 'We had a strange experience. Just before John died. I was in the garden and I heard his voice. He was saying 'Daddy, Daddy!' I heard it as clear as day. I don't mean to unnerve you, Michael, but you should think about what my wife has said.'

'Michael's faith will be with him. As it is with you.' said Macleod.

They took their leave, but Michael was perturbed. Perhaps John Fairbrother's last gesture was a signal to him. John was not asking him for help. He was trying to tell him something. He was pointing at him and mouthing a warning.

CHAPTER 9

THE ARDUOUS MEETING with Colonel Fairbrother had left Michael dispirited. He needed to find a way of exorcising the memories it had stirred up. He needed some light-heartedness, some *joie de vivre*. But where to find it? He had returned to his car without knowing where he was going.

The car seemed to gravitate in the direction of Mrs Weinstein's house. There was no conscious plan, simply an unusual surrender to impulse.

The rain had stopped, and Michael could hear laughter and shouts from the back garden, behind the driveway hedge. He approached, and at the risk of seeming intrusive, opened a gate without announcing himself at the front door.

Ruth was in the garden with Ben. They were hitting a ball on elastic with their tennis racquets. Ruth was deliberately clowning, unaware that Michael was watching. She dodged a wild ball, shrieking with mock fear. She stopped still when she saw the intruder, as if unsure how to react, and their eyes met in an unspoken recognition of feelings they could not reflect upon.

'You see, I told you it would stop raining! Would you like a walk in town? We could have lunch. I have the dog in the car', said Michael.

Michael knew about tactics. It was lucky he had the dog with him. The boy would not be able to resist.

Ben jumped up and down in excitement. He turned to his mother.

'Please, please, please, Mutti,' he said.

'What can I say?' said Ruth, smiling.

In town, the three of them slowly walked towards the café. Ben was making uneven progress, being pulled by the panting dog, and then being brought up sharply as the animal found something interesting to sniff.

Michael was proud to be walking with Ruth. She was elegant in a navy blue straw hat, set at an angle on her dark, shining hair. Her heels tapped out a jaunty rhythm on the pavement. Impulsively he asked her if she often visited Macleod. He wanted to know why she had been at his house on the rainy morning he had visited the Fairbrothers, Ruth lightheartedly evaded the question. 'We're just friends,' she said.

Suddenly Michael caught sight of Sarah and Vera, advancing purposefully towards them.

Sarah's obedient little Yorkshire terrier trotted beside her, desperately trying to keeps up with her long bouncing stride. Vera, in high heels, was, like the dog, at pains to keep up with her friend, taking three steps to Sarah's one.

'Michael! Just fancy seeing you here!' said Sarah. What are you up to?'

Just then, there was a loud growl from Toby, who was standing immobile as the terrier sniffed him. Suddenly Toby went for the small animal in a frenzy of snapping and snarling.

'O, my lord! Do something!' Sarah was screaming at Michael above the noise.

Michael grabbed the leash and tried to pull his dog away. It was no good. It looked as if Toby would kill Sarah's animal. He had to risk the jaws of both to separate them. The terrier was yelping and whining.

'Michael, what do you think you're doing bringing that brute out in public? Nimrod could have been killed. Look! He's shaking!'

Michael laughed.

'Poor little Nimrod. He falls short of being the mighty hunter he's named after. Maybe a name change is in order, I could suggest a few that would suit him better...' Sarah stamped her foot angrily.

'I don't know how you can discuss the name of my dog at a time like this. It's your fault, Michael. My dog could have been killed.'

She then glanced at Ruth with a look of undisguised hostility. A sly glint came into her eye.

'The least you can do now, Michael, is to take us for a drink,' she continued.

They made their way in awkward unison to the café, keeping the dogs apart, and tying them up, well away from each other, on a grassy verge. Michael felt disappointed they were now such a crowd. He wanted a peaceful excursion into town with Ruth.

The waitress, in black and white uniform, came to the table. She could have looked crisp, but her white headband sat askew on her head and her skirt hung loose and crooked from the waist. A sullen young woman, she licked her finger, before flicking her notepad to take the order.

'Just tea and sandwiches, then?' she said, mentally reckoning a disappointing tip.

Vera was looking in her compact mirror, powdering her nose, in an effort to restore calm after the dog fight.

Sarah was seated uneasily between Vera and Ruth. She turned abruptly to Ruth.

'How long are you staying here?' she asked.

Michael saw a fleeting look of defiance cross Ruth's face. She was not going to be upset by Sarah as she had been at the tennis court. 'It's my home for now. In some ways, it has always been my home,' she said.

Sarah either ignored or was oblivious to Ruth's irritation. 'What about your own parents? Don't you miss them?' she asked.

Michael cut in quickly. He was determined to support Ruth. 'I don't think Ruth wants to talk about that now, Sarah.'

'No, I don't mind,' Ruth said quietly. 'There's going to be a war, and it's safer for us to be out of Germany.'

Sarah let out a mirthless laugh to show her scorn of Ruth's assessment. 'I don't think there's going to be a war. Don't let's be so glum. Daddy says that even the Germans wouldn't be so stupid to go that far.'

'I am German'. The reply was understated, barely audible, but it provoked embarrassed silence. Michael straightened his cutlery, and Vera searched for some lipstick. Ruth continued. 'I have British citizenship, but I am, in many ways, German.'

'You'd better not say that too loudly,' said Sarah, looking at Michael and Vera for support.

'Mutti, do you think Toby should have some water?' said Ben.

Michael, glad of the distraction, called the waitress over.

'We don't serve dogs, sir', she said haughtily, before turning on her heel.

Sarah was undeterred, and continued her interrogation.

'I suppose you've had some problems here with anti-German feelings'.

'No, none. I've been here so often visiting my grandmother, staying many summers. I don't think my accent is so noticed'.

'Noticeable,' corrected Vera. Even she had seen Sarah's hostility to Ruth, thought Michael. She was trying to lighten the atmosphere. 'You're right, it isn't. By the way, your hat is very chic, Ruth. I must find one like it. Sarah, what do you think of my hat? It's not too tarty, is it?'

'It suits you very well,' said Sarah, crushing her friend with the double-entendre. Again she turned to Ruth.

'Do you like living in Camberley? I would imagine you feel more at home in London, where there are more people to share your religious celebrations, who understand your background. Don't you feel a little isolated here?'

'I don't, no. The majority of people have been very kind to Ben and me.'

Michael thought Ruth's reply was barbed, and he felt pleased at her spirit, but Sarah showed no understanding of Ruth's defiance. She went on with her relentless questions. 'How long have your family been in England?' asked Sarah.

'I think my grandparents came here just after they were married. I don't know.'

'That's wonderful. Maybe you have some male relatives here, then? I expect Ben misses male company?' said Sarah.

'I miss my dog, and he's a he,' said Ben. 'I miss grandmamma and grandpapa, too. They're looking after my dog.'

'Yes, dear!' Sarah tried a look of benevolence, but it sat unhappily on her face before it dropped away and she became thoughtful. Michael was reminded of her father's mask of benevolence after he had grabbed the child at the Garden Party. An uneasy thought came into his mind about inherited character traits. She continued, 'I expect you miss your daddy, too?' she said.

Ben looked towards his mother. Ruth looked uncomfortable. Michael saw that Sarah was not going to let an opportunity drop to drive a wedge between himself and her apparent rival, by expressing outrage, disapproval or social superiority. She also appeared to think that the mention of Ben's father would remind Michael of Ruth's unfortunate past.

Ruth was assertive. 'Your concern is touching, but I would prefer you address personal questions to me, not to Ben,' she said putting an arm round the boy who was looking nervously at Sarah. 'We need to leave in a minute'.

It was left, once more, to Vera to break the tension. It was Vera's way of defending Ruth, without having to offend anyone. She began a long, strange story about the countryside, when she had visited cousins. They too had beagles that Ben would have adored, she said, but they also had some other ghastly animals. She had found this out when she had gone on an excruciating country walk that the cousins had convinced her was 'healthy'. Not only did she not feel healthier afterwards, but she had ruined her Italian shoes and had sprained her ankle.

'I was immobilized in the drawing room, with my foot on a stool, and there they were. These two spaniels, putting their wet noses on me and, even more dreadful, smelling abominably. I couldn't get away.' She giggled. 'I don't suppose your dogs smell, do they, Ben? Germans are much too fastidious to tolerate that.'

Ben looked at her in total puzzlement, not knowing how to respond.

Sarah spoke to Vera like a parent explaining a simple truth to a young child. 'You're not a country girl; you're a Camberley girl, Vera. You fit so well in this community.' She turned to Ruth to pontificate. 'People here are surprisingly close-knit, Ruth. It's difficult for an outsider. Its square pegs in square holes in this town.'

Ruth looked at Sarah and her defiance seemed to fade. Michael hated bullying and even though he had to summon his courage, all he could manage to say was 'The trouble is, Sarah, that when all that you have is square pegs and square holes, life does get rather boring.'

Sarah shot an angry glance at Michael. 'While we're on the subject of misfits,' she said, glancing at Ruth, 'Daddy wants to see you as soon as possible.'

'I hope it's nothing serious. You're being secretive, Sarah' said Michael.

'There's some sort of a difficulty with Macleod, Sorry, can't say any more!' She referred to the vicar by his last name as though she were speaking of the under-gardener. She had the smug expression of one who has an excellent hand of cards and is about to lay them down on the table in triumph.

'You don't know the vicar, Ruth?' she continued.

Michael looked at Ruth inquisitively to see if she would now explain her acquaintance with the vicar, but she avoided a detailed answer.

'I do, yes! He has often come to the house. He has been a great help,' said Ruth.

Sarah looked sour. 'Doesn't surprise me', she said under her breath.

Ruth scraped her chair as she got up to leave. She was weary of the combative conversation. 'I must go now. So many questions have tired me.'

Michael tried to smooth over the awkwardness of the moment.

'Let me come with you, Ruth,' said Michael.

'No, please. I can look after myself. It looks like I have to, after all. Ben and I will find our own way home. Goodbye.'

Michael did not like the way she said 'goodbye'. It had a finality about it. He watched her as she left, holding Ben's hand, without a backward glance. He wanted to be with them. He felt he had failed them, somehow. He remembered the accusation Ruth had made against him in the rain, when he had met her outside Reverend Macleod's house. She had told him that he did not defend people when he saw an injustice. Just now he hated seeing Sarah attack her, and although he did try and support her, he had to admit it was inadequate. He felt annoyed with himself. Why did he find it so difficult to speak out? He had no difficulty recognizing even minor injustices, even when others did not seem to notice. Why could he not voice his feelings? He told himself that he had to find a way to make it up to her. It was not just that he had let her down, but somehow he felt he had also let himself down. He had to try and be more outspoken!

'O dear!' said Sarah lightly. 'She seems to have been offended. Did you see how she reacted when I mentioned Macleod?' she added. 'People are saying there is something going on between the two of them, but I shan't say any more. I'm not one to spread gossip, as you all know.'

Michael frowned.

'Don't look so unbelieving, Michael,' said Sarah. 'They've been seen going in and out of each other's houses. He is still a youthful-looking man and she – well, let's put it this way – she knows on which side her bread is buttered.'

'That's absurd!' said Michael, but he sounded downcast.

Sarah smiled. It was a smile that had a look of triumph.

CHAPTER 10

A DRAMA THAT WAS to affect the community, and Michael, was taking shape in an unlikely setting, Colonel Traverse's drawing room. The huge portrait of the colonel was hanging over them like an icon. 'It's bad enough facing one Traverse,' thought Michael as he sat in one of the uncomfortably hard chairs, 'but to be confronted by two of them ...'

The colonel was holding court to an all male company. Mr Bovis, the star-struck bank manager, was sitting on an upright chair, looking stiff and alert. By contrast Major Langton, a short, solid man in his sixties, with a large handle bar moustache, sat back on the sofa, a tumbler of whiskey in his hand. Next to him, Mr Manston, a red-headed man, smiled ingratiatingly at everyone. The mustachioed Langton was disconcerted by such affability. It smacked of insubordination. Instead of smiling back, he reciprocated with a deadpan, withering gaze.

The role and face of cool reason was adopted by Mr Reynolds, who always liked to look magisterial. He stood next to the sofa, and looked too rangy to be able to sit comfortably. The fronds of an ill-placed palm seemed in danger of tickling his chin as he folded his arms and frowned slightly at the gathering, like a disgruntled headmaster.

'Might as well get started' the colonel said brusquely.

Everyone had drifted in unhurriedly and Colonel Traverse, a stickler for punctuality, was irritated. 'We're late so I'll start. As you all know', he continued, 'Macleod has been head of our flock for a number of years.'

'Fifteen', said Mr Brown, with the rigor of the accountant that he was in daylight hours. Michael had known Mr Brown for many years, as much as anyone could know him. He was present at most Camberley functions, but seemed to dislike conversation – that is, his own conversation. He always seemed to be listening, though, and had the reputation of eavesdropping on any private talk at social gatherings, only skulking off when given a long hard stare by people who realised their confidences were overheard. Mr Brown was seated in a winged arm-chair, where he could sit back and be obscured from view, when necessary. He had earlier grumbled that he was not a willing participant at the meeting. 'I've had to endure a long day in the City and a rushed supper, but Colonel Traverse is not a man to be crossed,' he had said. Michael suspected his curiosity had led him here.

Brown corrected himself. 'He's been here fifteen and a half years, colonel.'

'Precisely!' Traverse shot him a glance of reprobation as, tortoise like, Brown retracted his head behind the armchair wings. Interruptions were as unwelcome as tardiness.

'Some of you may be unaware that something has come to light which makes it inappropriate for Macleod to continue in his position in this parish. I don't need to remind you that there is a strong military presence in this community, with our proximity to Sandhurst, and the Aldershot garrison. Not only that, but some feel, in error, that tensions have been raised by the threatening behaviour in Germany. We need a vicar who understands us, whom we can think of as our own, a man fit to lead.' His finger pointed skyward to emphasize a point. 'Some of us are born to lead and some of us aren't,' he said.

He paused. Gladys would have called it the dramatic pause in rehearsals, too short and the impact was thrown away. Too long, and the result was flat, like a collapsed soufflé. The colonel prided himself on his ability to rally men with his talk. The effect of his silence was ruined, though. The small family dog, who had so recently survived the ferocious jaws of Michael's dog, emerged from under a chair and began sniffing the colonel's shoes. The smell of them appeared to be very interesting and it wagged its tail enthusiastically. The colonel sneered and gave the animal a quick, sharp kick. It yelped in pain before retreating, tail between its legs, under a chair. Michael noticed everyone looking away, some barely suppressing a smile.

The colonel continued. 'It has been revealed to me that Macleod was a malingerer in the Great War. A shameful example of an officer and an Englishman!'

There was restlessness in the room. Reynolds shifted his weight from one foot to the other. Mr Brown retreated by sinking back between the obscuring wings of his armchair. Bovis' eyes shifted from one person to the next, trying to take his cue from others. Sitting on his high-backed chair with his beady eyes following the proceedings, he reminded Michael of a parrot on a perch.

Macleod was well-liked, and these accusations sat uncomfortably with the listeners. Only Michael, though, was prepared to speak. 'What evidence do you have, colonel?', he asked.

The colonel smiled, whether indulgent of Michael's question, or from malevolence, it was hard to tell. 'I heard it first through a comrade of his. A man in his regiment, who is nameless, for now. That's right! Ha! Ha! Code word nameless!'

The colonel's little joke perplexed Michael. 'Anything more specific to level against him?' he asked.

The colonel looked combatively at Michael.

'Well, yes, actually. I heard it from his own lips. Naturally he did not use the word 'malingerer', but he confirmed all the facts.'

'Would you mind outlining those to us, colonel?' said Mr Reynolds, looking impassive – a look he cultivated in his hope of appearing the older statesman. In fact he appeared more the dyspeptic teacher..

'Yes! Quite! He had to be relieved of his duties as an officer on the Western Front. He was invalided out of the army, but not with any wound. He was deemed mentally unfit for service'.

Major Langton stroked his moustache, ready to speak. He remembered the term used for a nervous disorder among soldiers. 'Shell shock. You mean he had shell shock.'

'Yes. That is, I'm not certain of the diagnosis, only that he was not up to the mettle of an officer,' said Traverse. The young Mr Manston, still eager and unable to stop smiling, decided to speak.

'I do see what you mean, colonel, sir. It does seem to be somewhat incompatible with his stewardship of this parish.'

'Exactly, Manston.' said Traverse.

Bovis suddenly spoke. 'An ouster. That's what's needed, Colonel Twaverse, sir. Ouster.'

The parrot likeness is getting stronger by the minute, thought Michael.

The colonel saw he had one supporter, but the others did not seem convinced. He tried his conciliatory tack, a little earlier than planned. He took up his debonair pose, and put one hand on his hip, and smiled.

'It's not as if I'm gunning for the man. I only think that it's time he moved on. His past is bound to come out now, and this is simply the wrong parish for him'

'The wrong pawish', echoed Bovis.

Michael tried to hide his indignation, as he spoke.

'With all due respect, sir, I think he's done a sterling job for 18 years, and I think we can be tolerant of some past weakness, if that is what it was.'

'Weakness?'

A tinge of red suffused the colonel's cheeks. He spluttered as he spoke.' No, not weakness. Failure to do his duty. Failure to come up to the mark of his fellow officers. A dereliction of his sworn duty.'

'Quite. Deweliction of duty,' said Bovis.

'I do see what you mean', said Langton, still stroking his whiskers, and muffling his comment behind his hand.

'I think it's a little bit exaggerated to get the fellow out on his ear, after all this time', said Reynolds.

'I confess, sir, I feel the same way,' said Michael. 'A forced move would devastate him. He would feel terrible shame. And besides, it would force him to move away from his daughters, and for what? He has a lot of supporters.'

'Yes,' said Reynolds. 'The reason for his move would soon come out and there is terrible prejudice against men who didn't do their duty in the Great War. Even after this time, many would shun him or even insult him to his face. Word would then spread to his new parish, and he would be a social outcast.'

'Listen!' There was a parade ground staccato edge to the colonel's voice now. He straightened his back as if to haul up some reserves of patience. It was not a resource he used often.

'The man has done all right here,' he continued. 'No one is tarnishing his reputation. I dare say there were a few sermons where he was very wide of the mark. You may remember when he seemed to support divorce. Talked about the mote in our own eyes. Bloody ridiculous! But apart from such incidents, he has, I agree, done a fairly satisfactory job. No! What I really find unacceptable is that here is a man who deserted his fellow officers and men at a time of utmost need. I won't mince my words. He chickened out.'

Here the colonel paused, but he quickly realized he had to use more persuasion.

'I know that there are probably reasons for his desertion. There must have been, or he would have been court-martialed or even shot. But the fact remains; he turned his back on his comrades. I'm not saying he should be hauled over the coals now. All I'm saying is that he should be transferred- quietly – to another parish. No fuss, no hoo-ha. His history, his entire attitude, jibes with this community.'

'It jibes. It vewy much jibes,' said Bovis, from his perch.

'I see what you mean, colonel,' said the eager-to-please Manston, looking around the room for other supporters.

'The colonel, as usual, is absolutely right,' continued Manston, 'He has to have the confidence of his parishioners, especially in these times. If things took a turn for the worse, and we had a lot of men on active duty in our numbers, he would be a disaster. I agree with the colonel. The situation can be handled quietly and amicably, and a transfer arranged.'

Michael disliked Manston intensely at that moment, but he suppressed his growing indignation, knowing he had to stay calm and reasoned to put his case forward.

'I'm sorry, gentleman, I must disagree,' he said. 'If the army discharged him with his honor intact, there can be no case against him. He is settled here, loved by many, with his two daughters and their children close by.'

'We're not talking about a legal case, Michael.' The colonel was raising his voice, now. 'We're just talking about a quiet transfer to a parish to which he would be better suited.'

The colonel noticed two outstretched legs protruding from the winged armchair.

'Brown!' he said sharply. 'I haven't heard your take on it yet.'

The legs withdrew slowly, and the face of Mr Brown, still wizened by a long day's work in the City, peered form behind an armchair wing like a frightened fox cub peering out of its den.

'Yes, yes! I can see your point, colonel.' Ever the accountant, he had a suggestion. 'Perhaps a vote would be in order. Let's take a count.'

The colonel could not hide his exasperation with the assembly. 'I was coming to that!' he said.

'First I would like to know how you would affect the transfer', said Reynolds, as he stood over them with that same magisterial look.

'It's quite, simple', said the colonel. 'I happen to know the Bishop of Guildford personally. I would set up a meeting with him, and would like a volunteer to join me. Langton, perhaps you would come with me? It would then be a matter of making a few suggestions and presenting a signed petition from some of the more prominent members of the parish.'

Michael felt he had to speak out. Much as he had little regard for authority, he found it extremely stressful to speak out in a situation such this. He had to say something, he couldn't leave his friend in the lurch, He stumbled over his reply. 'I'm sorry, sir. Isn't there some other way? Canon Macleod is a friend of mine, and I have known him since I was a boy. I must tell you that I find this rejection of him is not what he deserves.' He realised his words lacked force, and paled after the Colonel's barrage.

The colonel was contemptuous. 'I'm sorry you feel that way, Rogers. I thought that, as a soldier, you would understand, but clearly you do not. You are entitled to your opinion, but let us keep emotion out of it, shall we? Can we have a vote, please, gentlemen? Those who agree with me raise your hands and say 'Aye'.'

Langton took a quick gulp of whiskey from his tumbler and held it up as if to say, 'Cheers!'

'Aye!'

Manston and Bovis immediately followed. Reynolds shifted un-comfortably on his feet before assenting and an arm stuck up from the winged armchair, before darting back into obscurity.

'That seems to be settled. I'll let you know when we meet the bishop,' said Traverse.

'And remember! Bishops are addressed as 'Your Grace'. Protocol, you know. Mustn't forget protocol. Makes them sound like bloody balleri-nas, though, doesn't it? Ha! Ha!'

The self-appointed adjudicator, the rangy Mr Reynolds, spoke out. 'It's an archbishop, not a bishop, you address as 'Your Grace', colonel.'

'Rubbish!' said Traverse.

Michael was exasperated. 'If you'll excuse me,' said Michael, not dis-guising the sharpness in his voice. He was unable to find the words to question Traverse's persecution of Macleod. Without looking at anyone and with only a brief nod at the assembly, he left the room. He was ap-palled at the vote to take action against Canon Macleod. He wondered how a group of intelligent men could follow Traverse' exhortations with so little questioning. Could they not see the unnecessary cruelty of their action? It was as if there was some primal herd mentality that was com-ing into play, a hunting instinct to follow the leader after the prey. He had seen the same herd mentality on the newsreels, with Germans in thrall to that wild-eyed Herr Hitler.

Canon Macleod was a sensitive man. It was difficult to imagine him in the trenches in France. He thought of the sadness such disloyalty among his flock would cause him. He thought of his daughters, known to everyone as neighbours who lived close by and who were such a com-fort to their father. He would have to take action to thwart Traverse, at the risk of alienating his circle, and perhaps even Sarah. 'I must do something,' he said to himself. 'I don't quite know what, but I will do something.'

His resolve weakened as he thought of Sarah. He felt uneasy. His head-to-head with her father was going to make his relationship with her awkward. She would be coming to India with Vera. His life seemed so untidy. How could he think of Sarah and be so preoccupied with thoughts of Ruth? Yet he was only allowing himself a little flirtation with a pretty woman. They both knew it was hopeless – he was engaged, she was a mother and of a different religion, he was based thousands of miles away, and about to return. No one was deceiving themselves. His relationship with Sarah would not change. It would progress without any effort of his part, sanctioned by the whole community. The only action he needed to take now was to protect Macleod from persecution.

MICHAEL DREADED THE MEETING with Canon Macleod. He was glad Macleod had agreed to meet him that same night, after the colonel's get-together, and at the vicarage, where Macleod could feel more comfortable. But he was very surprised when Macleod greeted him with a smile and warmly shook his hand. He was even more affable than usual. He thought wryly that Macleod might have been helping himself to a few nightcaps; not that he could blame him after all the trouble that was brewing for him in the community. But he knew the canon was a man of probity; that was the irony. A lesser man would help himself to Dutch courage and actively enlist all the help he could muster. Yet here was Michael, his lone defender, and he had come on his own initiative.

Macleod was apologizing for being unable to use the drawing room. Michael had requested privacy, and a visiting daughter was in that room. He led the way to his study where bookcases lined the walls from floor to ceiling. There was a large desk, piled high with papers so that not an inch of surface was visible, and Macleod had to clear paperwork off the small armchairs before they could sit down. He motioned Michael to sit, while he poured two generous glasses of sherry at a side table. Michael took a deep breath before speaking.

'It's not such a happy mission I'm on,' he said.

Macleod was unfazed even by this announcement as he handed Michael the brimming glass and sat down.

'Don't mind that, Michael. Just tell me what's on your mind.'

'You must be aware of what Colonel Traverse is up to,' said Michael.

Macleod raised his eyebrows slightly and nodded. He looked strangely impassive.

'I wanted you to know that I don't like it and I will help you to fight your corner,' said Michael.

Macleod laughed unexpectedly. 'Fight?' he said. 'That's not what I do best, you know!'

Macleod's dismissive reaction irritated Michael.

'I mean defend yourself,' he said. 'You have to do something. You can not sit back and watch your reputation being dragged through the mud.'

Macleod leaned back comfortably into the armchair.

'There's nothing much to say, is there Michael?'

'What do you mean?' said Michael. There's plenty to say. You have to defend your record in the Great War. You had shell shock. There's nothing dishonorable about that! I've seen it myself. I've seen men kill themselves when their minds have gone after the shock of battle. There's nothing to be ashamed of.'

'No. There's no need to be ashamed. But I'm not going to change those men and their attitudes. You see, it wasn't just shell shock.'

Michael looked at him sharply. He was not in the mood for nasty revelations.

'You see, Michael, the colonel and his men are right. My attitude did change in the trenches. They would say, I suppose, that I turned soft.'

Michael did not want to hear the confessions of a man he viewed as a father figure. He wanted to defend him and to feel it was right to defend him. He had an impulse to end the interview there and then but Macleod continued, and he had to listen.

'This will shock you, but had I known at the beginning of the war what I knew at the end, I would have been a conscientious objector.'

Michael sighed. No soldier liked to hear those words. They were still linked to cowardice, even though the men who evaded service in this way had to suffer for their choice. During the Great War, the 'conchies', had to endure cruel interrogations, imprisonment and hard labour – not that any of this could restore their reputation in the eyes of the public. They were still tainted by their refusal to enlist. Michael had always dismissed them as a fringe group of flawed individuals. Now his mentor was allying himself to their cause. It was as though Macleod was scorning his offer of support.

'Don't misunderstand me,' said Macleod. 'I respected the men I was fighting with. More than respected them, I loved them. Even when they died horrible deaths, even though our cause was murky, there was nobility about the way they laid down their lives. It's difficult to explain how I changed. I suddenly saw the big picture.'

The anger was bubbling up inside Michael. He had never thought he could feel such resentment towards Canon Macleod, and he could not suppress the growing rage. He wished Macleod would show some sadness, even shed some tears, anything but this somber reasoning. He was almost shouting when he answered.

'You're talking to a soldier. A soldier who believes in what he is doing. You're talking pacifist drivel. Don't you think I have a mission? Don't you think I want to do some good, serving as a soldier? '

Macleod looked down and did not answer him for a while. When he did speak, it was in that irritatingly gentle tone of voice that he had used all evening.

'My faith came back to me on the battlefield, Michael,' he said. 'There was no argument I could make to God's commandment 'Thou shalt not kill'. Four small words. They're pretty uncompromising, aren't they?'

'No!' said Michael. 'No, they are not! You were fighting a ghastly, belligerent regime in the Great War. I am fighting killers, rapists, looters on the Northwest frontier. It's not easy and that is why I am proud of what I do!'

Michael paused, waiting for Macleod's answer, but there was silence, and Michael continued. 'They're barbarians, those Pathan. You should know. You conducted John Fairbrother's memorial service. Don't tell me that his death didn't make you sick. It made me sick. You know what?' Michaels's voice was trembling with emotion. 'I want to go back there. I want to go back to India to bury as many of those bastards that killed John as I can.'

He suddenly stopped. He realised he had gone too far.

'I'm ... I'm sorry Canon Macleod. I shouldn't have used those words. It's just that after the campaigns that I've been through lately, I ... well! ... I get pretty heated.'

'I understand,' said Macleod. 'I understand more than you know.'

'Are you just going to leave it at that then?' snapped Michael.

'You feel a lot of hatred, don't you, Michael?'

Michael shrugged. 'I suppose you could call it hatred' he conceded.

'You despise the Pathan, do you Michael?'

'Put it this way, I have no respect for them.'

There was silence for a long time. Michael's words seemed to hang in the air, unchallenged Then Macleod spoke.

'Remember the story of the Samaritan woman in the Bible, Michael? She was the foreigner, the outsider. That's what Samaritans were to the Jews in those days. Not only that, she was a loose woman who had to go to the well in the heat of the day, when there would be no one to point fingers at her. But it was she who impressed the Lord with her faith. It's easy to feel compassion for your peers, but to love your enemy? That's the difficult thing! Michael, you're in for a shock.'

'What do you mean?' asked Michael.

'I mean that something is going to transform that anger of yours. Your hatred is too raw, it's too sorrowful. I've seen it before.'

Michael's look was accusing. 'What do you mean, you've seen it before? You've never seen me like this until tonight.'

'I've seen it before,' repeated Macleod. 'In myself!'

A feeling of discomfort had become unbearable and Michael stood up. He would work behind the scenes to help Macleod. He would try to reconcile the community as much as he could. But this interview had been useless. He wondered how it had become an examination of his beliefs. He had to get away, quickly.

'I'm sorry, Canon Macleod. I really must go now. I came here to warn you about the slanders against you. I've done that. Thank you for seeing me at such short notice.'

He stuck out his hand for a formal handshake, and was disconcerted when Canon Macleod clasped him warmly in an embrace. He was embarrassed to see that Macleod's eyes were moist. He did not want to be confronted with Macleod's emotional nature now.

'I will be praying for your reconciliation, Michael,' he said, 'For you to find peace once more. Don't be afraid to be an island, Michael. An island in a sea of unthinking prejudice.'

Michael's anger returned. He could not help it. 'I'm not a maverick. Don't cast me in the role of a rebel. I don't want to strike out on my own. Can't you understand that, Reverend?'

'You might not know it, but you are already with the outsiders,' said Macleod.

It was such a strange thing to say, thought Michael, as Macleod led him out to the front door and he passed into the night.

CHAPTER 12

'HELLO RUTH.'

The voice on the other end of the telephone sounded surprised, wary.

'Michael?'

Michael felt nervous.

'Listen, I wondered if you could come to the pictures with me this week. There's a film with Fred Astaire, which is supposed to be fun, and I didn't have a chance to talk to you over tea.'

'No. Thank you. I feel tired.'

It was obvious that she was still smarting from Sarah's interrogation in the café.

'Sarah and Vera can be too talkative, but they try to be friendly,' said Michael.

There was a silence.

'Is there any evening or afternoon you could be free? The film starts at 2 o'clock, or seven.'

There was a pause. 'Afternoon would be better.'

'Friday?'

Whatever Ruth had felt, she had agreed. He would make amends for Sarah's behavior on Friday. It was his duty to do so. Michael hoped no one would see them. He did not want anyone to have the wrong impression.

He stood at Ruth's door, slightly earlier than he was expected. Ruth herself answered, her hat sitting obliquely on her face, partially hiding her face. She was adjusting her white gloves, unable to look directly at her escort.

'I have the car waiting,' said Michael. It was a stupid thing to say. The engine was running noisily, and it was just behind him in the driveway. The shadowing brim of Ruth's hat could not hide her smile.

There was no-one near the cinema. The weather was too good to sit in the dark, and the only other customers were a couple of young girls, and a group of middle aged matrons. Nonetheless, Michael was glad of the dark anonymity of the interior, and he felt free to enjoy the intimacy of sitting next to Ruth on the plush velvet seats.

The Pathé newsreel announced itself with a crowing cockerel, and the reassuring voice of the commentator was jaunty. But then the tone changed. Austria was in mourning. A group of eight Nazis entered the Chancellery building in Vienna and gunned down the Austrian Chancellor, Dollfuss in an attempted coup d'etat. Dollfuss had recently banned the Austrian Nazi Party which was intent on annexing Austria to Germany. Michael glanced at Ruth. She was holding her hands in front of her mouth, as if shocked or suppressing a gasp. She whispered hoarsely, 'What will make these Nazis stop?' Michael acted instinctively. He took hold of her wrist, guiding her hand gently into his. They sat, hand in hand, looking at the screen, but Michael now felt indifferent to the film, as the warmth of her hand melted all remaining formality. Ruth seemed to be comforted. When the scene changed, they were still joined, their fingers now entwined.

When they left the cinema, Michael cared little who would see them. They were arm in arm, and agreed to drive to a hotel in Guildford, where they could relax over a cream tea.

The hotel was an old posting house, with a sign for livery stables over the courtyard archway. The lounge was a comfortable paneled room, with chintz-covered armchairs and monochrome prints of hunting scenes on the walls.

Michael felt buoyant, almost drunk with the new-found intimacy. Ruth, however, was distracted and the smile she returned was strained.

'That newsreel upset you, didn't it?' said Michael.

'It's not just that horrible event, Why do so few people stand up to the Nazis?' 'Dollfuss did support the Jews and took a stand against the Nazis and I admire him for that, but most people let them do what they want'. I just heard that two weeks ago, the German Undersecretary of Transport, Erich Klausener was gunned down in the same way in Berlin.

A week earlier he had publicly criticized Hitler. He must have known that they wouldn't let him live for long. But why are there not more like him? Is everyone scared or do they just close their eyes to it because it doesn't affect them?'

Michael became pensive. He suddenly felt guilty about his recent failure to support Ruth. 'I think people may want to speak out but get intimidated. You have to feel deeply about something and have courage. I'm not sure I would have spoken out like that.'

'Most people would not, that's the tragedy,' said Ruth. 'Unless you really believe that what you are standing for, matters more than your life, you would not - most people either value their lives too much or don't have the inner fire that doesn't allow them to remain silent. Many in Germany have a blind loyalty to authority, especially all those men in uniform.'

'But the whole chain and structure of command in the armed forces depends on loyalty. Discipline depends on loyalty. Disloyalty is one of the worst sins you can commit in the army.'

Ruth looked straight at him, 'Would you never be disloyal?'

'Disloyal to whom? To my regiment? To my friends? To you? '

There was sharpness in her reply. 'You tell me, Michael. I've seen enough disloyalty to last a lifetime,' said Ruth.

Michael did not expect her reply. He was stung by her mistrust, but he suddenly thought of Ben, and the mysterious, absent father. He then guessed that Ruth was speaking from bitter experience and he felt calmer. 'I've only been disloyal once, that I can remember. I reported a fellow officer. He was a nasty piece of work and gave out humiliating punishments. One day I couldn't take his behavior any more. He made one soldier stand to attention in the heat of the day because his shoes were unpolished. Torture under the Indian sun. The man stood there for hours until we saw his legs buckle under him. He was delirious and had to be taken to the sanatorium with heat exhaustion. I went straight to a senior officer. '

'That doesn't sound disloyal of you, to alert people to a bully!'

'The officer I approached thought so. He asked me if I knew what I was doing. He put it this way. 'What would you do if a private came to you to complain against a sergeant?' I said I would see it as a weakness in the soldier. My own words suddenly made me understand what I had done.'

The effects of his words on Ruth surprised Michael. She became agitated and her voice grew louder.

'That's what Herr Hitler would tell his soldiers. You know the real traitors, though? The ones who are dragging Germany into the mud. The spies, the finger-pointers, the ones ready to stone their own neighbours. My country has gone. Its name has been blackened for ever by blind, faithful followers. Loyalty isn't justice. It shouldn't be blind.'

Michael suddenly realized that the room had gone quiet. He saw people staring at Ruth. A man in a dark suit approached, a manager.

Ruth looked down biting her lip and frowning to control her emotion. Michael felt his admiration of her grow. The suited man leaned over to speak discreetly to Michael.

'If you don't mind, sir. We try to keep things quiet and relaxed in this room. I'm sure you understand.'

'Quite so,' said Michael. 'We'll turn down the volume.'

'I'm sorry,' said Ruth.

'No, you're right, Ruth. Loyalty has to be questioned. Always.'

They were silent for a moment, then Michael asked, 'Do you miss Germany?'

Michael really wanted to know if she missed Ben's father, that shadowy rival he knew so little about.

'I miss the Germany I used to know. Our chalet in the mountains, picnics with my family in the meadows, opening the shutters in the morning to see the steam rising from the forests on the mountain. It seems primeval. You feel so small, insignificant, but in a good way. I wish I could take you there.' She smiled and spoke with irony. 'Some other time, of course!'

'That's enough about Germany and me, I know so little about you, Michael. Tell me about India!'

'Where do you want me to start?'

'Everything. What you do when you get up in the morning. Who your friends are. Are you ever in danger? What makes you laugh?'

'I think I'll take what makes me laugh,' he said

'It was embarrassing. I was in India, waiting on a parade ground on horseback for a gun salute to mark the New Year. I had just bought the pony I was on but it was dancing around and becoming very frisky.'

'I didn't know you rode. Very dashing,' said Ruth.

He enjoyed the compliment, and continued. 'I thought I knew how to ride. But you know what pride comes before? Anyway, this horse stepped sideways and into the colonel on his mount. It crushed his leg, and he just stood there on his horse, stock still, glaring angrily at my pony until he couldn't take it anymore.' Michael stopped and looked questioningly at Ruth.

'Go on.'

'So this colonel told me to get off my horse and to take his.'

'I have a feeling that the colonel is not going to be able to count on your pony's loyalty,' said Ruth.

Michael smiled. He liked the idea of conspiring with Ruth and continued his story.

'No sooner was he on the animal, than the guns went off and so did my horse, with the colonel hanging on to the mane, shouting, 'Won't somebody shoot this effing animal?' '

Michael felt he could have been saying anything. What was important was left unsaid as their eyes met.

'Did the horse stop?'

'It did, and very suddenly. But the colonel didn't. His whole bulk – he was rather chubby – became airborne over the horse's neck.'

'He must have been furious.'

'It's strange. He came out with some very ripe swear words, but he seemed to see the funny side of it. Certainly everybody else did! There's a lot of camaraderie in the army.'

Ruth smiled and they looked at each other, continuing the same unspoken conversation that had run in parallel with their spoken words.

Michael hesitated to speak more openly about himself, but the headiness of being so physically close to her persuaded him to continue.

'I've felt on my own, lately, in spite of the fellowship I find in the army. I have this strange feeling that I'm an outsider whether I'm in India or in England.'

'An outsider? How can that be? I'm the outsider, Michael. I'm German, I'm Jewish, and I'm a lone parent.'

'I haven't told anyone else this, Ruth, but I no longer have any faith in what I am doing in India. If it wasn't for something personal I have promised to do in India, I don't think I would return. I used to have pride in what we are doing out there, but "For King and Country" doesn't mean much to me any more. I dare not say anything to the other officers there, they are totally committed to what we are doing. And I am at odds with people here in Camberley as everyone expects me to be proud and happy to be in my regiment. So, you see, I'm a bit like you.'

Ruth looked at him. Her eyes met his intense gaze. Then she did something unexpected. She suddenly leaned towards him and kissed him on the cheek. It was a gesture that meant more to him at the time than any fervent embrace.

He smiled and squeezed her hand.

'I fear the future, Ruth'

'What do you have to be afraid of?'

'Of never seeing you again after I leave'

'You shouldn't talk like that. You have other priorities.'

Michael leaned towards her and spoke softly. 'No, Ruth, you are my priority. You know what I said about not fitting in here? Well that goes for Sarah too. I have known and liked Sarah for a long time, but I am now starting to see her as part of the Camberley establishment, and not someone I could spend the rest of my life with.'

Ruth looked down at the table, not betraying any emotion.

'Ruth, soon I'll be a long way off in the foothills of the Himalayas. When I sit in the officers' mess, looking out from a huge window facing the peaks, I have always longed for some one to share the experience with me. Now I know who that 'someone' is. If only you could come with me! '

Michael took hold of Ruth's hand again. 'Listen. Let's stay for dinner here. We can go for a stroll in town, and I can buy a shirt and white tie for the meal. I could even rent a room.' He corrected himself suddenly. 'Rooms. We could use them to freshen up. What do you think?' 'I don't want this evening to end,' said Michael. 'I want to be with you all the time.'

This time Ruth was silent. Then she spoke softly. 'I know,' she said. 'I know because I feel the same way. But Michael, we have to be sensible. You will be leaving soon and you'll be away for a year and a half. Just now my main concern is to make Ben's future secure. I can't do anything to jeopardise that. You will have time to think while you are out in India.'

'But Ruth! You can't think that I could ever change my mind about you! The last thing I'd do is hurt you, Ruth. I will sort out the situation with Sarah. Please, let's just follow our hearts.'

'Michael right now, it's better if we just do what is expected of us, that I fall in with my grandmother's plans, that you continue your engagement. I'm tired and I need time to think. Please let's just go home now'

The car's headlights lit up the tall hedgerows as the car wound through the deep country lanes. They were silent. Occasionally Michael would grasp Ruth's hand and look quickly at her. He only grew nervous as the car's tyres crunched over the gravel on her grandmother's driveway.

'Ruth, what plans does your grandmother have for you?' She hesitated. Her hand rested on the handle of the car door.

'Telephone me.'

The car did not start until well after the front door had closed. Michael was lost in thought.

CHAPTER 13

I've just heard some very interesting gossip.'

Gladys heaved her heavy wicker shopping basket on to the kitchen table with a sigh of relief.

Michael stopped polishing his shoe for a moment, holding the brush in mid air. He quickly realized his mother was too calm for his tryst with Ruth to have been discovered,

'Michael, you really should let Mrs Waller do that.'

She turned her head toward Mrs Waller, who was busy peeling vegetables at the sink.

'Waller. Please put these away when you've finished peeling. We have some tasty marmalade made by Mrs Rutherford. I was lucky to get it. A Madeira cake from goodness knows who, and someone's freshly-picked rhubarb for a delicious crumble.'

She glanced at Michael to see if he had taken the bait. ·

Feigning indifference, Michael nonchalantly continued to buff his shoe.

'What gossip?'

'It seems that Ruth from over the road made a very bad alliance with Ben's father'

Mrs Waller's voice could be heard as she bent over the sink, as if talking to herself.

'Such a nice girl, that Ruth!'

'Did you say something, Waller?' said Gladys with irritation in her voice.

'No, madam. Nothing.'

'Now Michael,' continued Gladys, 'I don't know whether she married him or not, but either way her parents are in some kind of danger because of him. He has a high ranking position in the National Socialist Party, and even knows Herr Hitler. You know what an embarrassment Ruth and her family would be to him. Mrs Weinstein is trying to persuade the parents to leave Germany, but they are stubborn, and want to wait until this whole thing has blown over. She's trying to distance the family from Ben's father, and so is desperately trying to match-make for Ruth. A young investor, a friend of the family, has been invited down on the pretext of selling her some stock.'

'O heck,' said Mrs Waller, still bending over the sink

'Gladys was angry. 'Waller, did you say something?'

'No, madam. It's only that these here vegetables are ever so difficult to peel.'

Gladys glanced at her son, and he realized from her look that she knew more about his feeling for Ruth than he had guessed. He felt anger, not knowing if it was at his mother's duplicity, or his resentment of the young guest at Ruth's house.

'Do you know Mrs Weinstein well?'

'I've known her for years. Very pleasant, cultured; books everywhere in the house, and from a very well-established family. But of course there will always be a distance between us, because she's Jewish. I believe they're even bringing Ben up to be Jewish, though obviously his father is not. I expect Ruth will marry some nice respectable man of her own faith, here in England, and all will resolve itself.'

The purpose of Gladys's conversation was obvious, but that did not matter to her.

She was relieved, however, when she heard the front door closing and the approach of a woman in heels. The kitchen door was flung open, and without stopping for breath Estelle burst into the kitchen, and Michael heard Mrs Waller, a great fan of his aunt, mumble, 'About time, too!'

'Hello! It's only me!'

'Only me!' thought Michael. 'Typical of Aunt Estelle's false modesty.'

He thought of the time when she had said, 'I just thought I'd treat myself to a little something, and then had shown off a very expensive mink, that was so unsparing in its cut, it swayed as she walked. Or when she had said her husband had given her a small token of his devotion. She had then pointed out of the window to a princely Bentley, strategically parked in the driveway. In fact the only time this ersatz humility was not present was when misfortune had befallen her. A mere head cold would then become a huge burden and no detail was spared as to her suffering and courage.

'Michael! What's this I hear about you? You're in some kind of trouble.'

The discomfort Michael felt was obvious, and he kept silent. He assumed his aunt was talking about his meeting with Ruth. It would now be very awkward when he saw her, with everyone's eyes on them.

'Gladys,' continued his aunt, 'I've just heard all about it.'

'Whatever can you mean, Estelle? Do take that ridiculous fox fur off. It's the middle of summer, and I'm not sure I like a dead animal getting close to my food.' Gladys sounded flippant, but she could not mask the look of alarm on her face.

Yet the news had to be good because Estelle was not in the mood for arguing with her sister. She turned instead to Michael. 'Terence would have been so proud of you, as would your father. When I married Terence I knew he was a man of great integrity. He had had little peccadilloes – what man hasn't?'

Michael thought she shot him a meaningful glance after this rhetorical question, but we couldn't have been happier', she continued. 'It was to be our thirtieth wedding anniversary this month.' Her eyes started to water.

'I know we were never blessed with children, but. . .'

Michael was impatient. 'Please, aunt, tell me what I am supposed to be proud of.'

'Yes. . . .well' sniffed Estelle, snapping her handbag as she brought out a handkerchief. 'It's about Canon Macleod. Michael is in bad odor with certain gentlemen of the parish because he has been defending him. It's put another way, of course. They say that Michael is not helping the parish to progress. There is even some ridiculous notion (I have it from our very own Lady Bracknell, Dora Cunningham) that Michael is not taking his religion seriously, and can not take decisions about our priest, because he has taken an interest in Judaism and our Jewish fraternity.'

Michael was angry. 'That is offensive,' he said. 'I suppose we're all going to be tainted by that crazed Mr Hitler; and the intolerance he spouts'.

'Shh. Don't say so!' said Gladys. 'It's extremely rude to single out your friendship with the Weinstein's, but never compare us to the Germans.'

'I don't want a political discussion, but please, aunt, tell me what is being said about Canon Macleod.'

'They're saying he was a coward and a malingerer in the Great War.'

'This has got to stop. It has gone too far. I want to go and speak to Colonel Traverse.'

'Shouldn't you stay out of it dear', said Gladys. 'Estelle, why do you put things in his head. You know that colonel Traverse is behind this and it could interfere with Michael's relationship with Sarah'

Estelle smiled. 'He always does the right thing. Just like Terence.'

Michael went into the hallway, to grab his trilby on his way out. His certainly didn't feel he deserved his aunt's praise. His mother and aunt stood in the kitchen looking at each other questioningly, for once at a loss for words.

CHAPTER 14

THE EVENING LIGHT was growing dim but Michael could see Colonel Traverse had a smile on his face as he rang the doorbell of the vicarage. Michael had asked Traverse to meet with himself and Canon Macleod. He wanted to defuse the campaign that Traverse had launched against Macleod, to settle matters. So the three men were meeting.

But Traverse' strange smile was out of place. It did not augur well. It reminded Michael of the time Traverse had rebuked a child so cruelly at the garden party and his inappropriate smile then. Michael noticed that Colonel Traverse was always impatient and now, as they waited, his behaviour became more and more peculiar. He kept lifting himself up and down on his heels, as if he were an athlete limbering up for the start of a race. 'Can't pull the wool over my eyes.' he said. Michael recoiled at the colonel's words which showed such an open distrust of Macleod. 'Brigadier once told me "Nothing gets past you Traverse. Not one damn thing." ' Michael found it oddly satisfying that the hidden barb of the officer's words seemed to have escaped the colonel, who carried on talking. 'Never been fleeced. No flies on me. Ha! Ha!'

The language of the farmyard was becoming hard to bear, and Michael was relieved when the door was answered by Macleod, who greeted them warmly. But as he fussed about their raincoats in the hallway, and looked from one to the other, Michael could see he was nervous.

'You're both well, I hope. Good, good! The housekeeper has the day off, but I have some sherry and sandwiches in the drawing room.'

It was typical of Macleod, thought Michael, to prepare a welcoming snack. It made him feel guilty about the purpose of his visit.

The drawing room was large and untidy, yet this made it all the more relaxed and inviting. Papers and books were on every surface. Pictures were not quite straight on the walls, and the potted plants by the window seemed to be growing out of control. Instead of the usual dour prints of hunting scenes and amateur daubings of the suburban wall, portraits of children and holiday photographs were hung on every available space. Michael's gaze was drawn to one large photograph resting on the grand piano. It was of a smiling woman with a plump baby on her knee. Michael recognised Mrs Macleod, as he had known her as a boy.

'Sit down, gentlemen. Make yourselves comfortable.'

Michael was about to sink into a huge sofa, when he noticed he was about to sit on a similarly outsized cat. It was sleeping, oblivious to its peril.

'That's Chivers, like the marmalade,' said Macleod. 'Hope you don't mind cats. Help yourselves to the sandwiches. We don't stand on ceremony here.'

Michael sat on the sofa, and seemed to sink down into to its sumptuous down-filled cushions.

The colonel found the only hard-backed chair in the room. He looked uncomfortable, as he sat with a ramrod straight back. He cleared his throat before speaking. 'We'd better get down to business, if you don't mind' he said.

'Yes. Of course. Please begin,' said Macleod.

'As you know' began the colonel,' people have been a little concerned about your war record. We just want to straighten things out.'

Macleod was still congenial. 'What would you like to know, colonel?'

'You could start by telling us where you were in action and who you were with in the Great War.'

'I was with the First Lincolnshire Battalion. We were in the Somme.'

'What a terrible place to have been,' said Michael. 'The losses must have been appalling.'

'Our battalion lost over 240 men in 24 hours at one point,' said Macleod. His composure was broken and he looked pained. 'I really don't see why this is relevant.'

'Let's just press on for the moment,' said Traverse. 'How would you describe your record there?'

'I don't think you served in France?' said Macleod. It was the first time Michael saw him irritated. His question embarrassed Traverse, and he reddened.

'I was very shaken by it,' Macleod continued. 'The men were often no more than boys. They cried out for their mums and dads as they died.'

'You said you were shaken?' said the colonel.

'I was close to despair. I would really rather not talk about it.'

The colonel was unyielding in his interrogation.

'So what did you do?' he asked.

'Do?' said Macleod. 'There was nothing I could do. That was the trouble. There was one young man, a Private aged 17. He had an appalling wound in his side. The medics could not get to us because of the line of fire. I tried my best to give him some first aid.' Macleod stopped talking.

'Did it work?' asked Michael.

The vicar did not seem to hear the question. He was looking down, nervously squeezing the tips of his fingers.

'I held his head in my lap all night. I said the Lord's Prayer again and again, like a mantra. The guns wouldn't stop. The earth was shaking beneath us with every explosion. I thought, 'I only have to wait till morning. If he lives until sunrise, he'll be all right.' '

Michael could see Macleod was upset. His voice was becoming softer, as if he were talking to himself, his eyes were damp and seemed to redden Michael did not know how to interrupt him. He wished he had not come. The vicar continued, his voice becoming more and more quiet, until Michael had to strain to hear him.

'His breath grew labored. Then at dawn, he clasped at me, as if he were drowning. He looked at me, thinking I had an answer. As if I could do something. I was useless. Helpless. Why was he dying and not me?' He stopped and when he next spoke he sounded angry. 'I should have died, not he' he said. At last he looked up at his visitors, but there was no sign of resentment that had been in his voice; just an expression of sadness on his face.

The colonel cleared his throat again and spoke out.

'What we wanted to know, Macleod, was how your service ended.'

'After that incident I began to shake violently,' said Macleod. 'I thought it was the cold. I couldn't stop it. I couldn't sleep. Pictures kept coming into my mind to torment me, images of death. I thought it was the end of the world, the end of civilization.' He paused again and added very quietly, 'I thought it was the end of God.'

Michael understood at once.

'You had shell shock,' he said.

'Wait a moment!' said the colonel. 'I happen to know that the British army ruled in, let me see… in 1922 that there was no such thing as shell shock!'

Michael realized that the colonel had been expecting the vicar's answers, and had already prepared a response.

'I was lucky,' said Macleod. 'I had an enlightened doctor, Captain McDowell. He was on the Medical Board that heard my case. He later became a famous psychologist.'

'You know what happened to others like you, don't you?' said the colonel.

'Yes!' replied Macleod. 'Some walked straight into enemy fire. Others turned their revolvers on themselves. There were some who were executed by our own men.'

Michael was surprised how Macleod could talk about such things without becoming very emotional. The colonel seemed to have a strange effect on him. He seemed to be concentrating, almost as if he were preaching, as he answered the colonel's questions and it seemed to help him to remain reasonably calm.

'Yes! And executed for what?' asked the colonel. He answered his own question. 'For cowardice.'

Michael wanted to stop the interview. He looked at Macleod, and was again surprised to see him unfazed.

'So what happened then?' asked the colonel.

'Hospitalised. Sent to a convalescent home for neurasthenics in Craiglockhart, Scotland. Known as Dottyville in the army. Then discharged from the service.'

The colonel sneered. 'You were invalided out for mental reasons?'

'You could say that,' Macleod replied.

'And your brother officers either had to see the war out or be laid to rest under a white cross.' The colonel was trembling with anger, his emotions were barely under control.

'Steady on, colonel!' said Michael.

'No. I want this sorted out once and for all,' said the colonel.

'It was a medically valid reason, colonel,' said Michael. 'I think the vicar had given us enough explanations, and I'm perfectly satisfied with them. In fact I salute his war record.'

Traverse frowned. 'Michael, you're speaking out of turn,' said the colonel. 'I'm sorry, Macleod. I don't like this, but I have to say it. I've never shied away from speaking my mind and doing the right thing.'

Macleod listened impassively. The colonel continued.

'I do not understand why someone like yourself, with your record, should be in a largely military parish. Many agree with me,' continued Traverse.

Macleod looked straight at the colonel.

'I'm committed to this parish, one hundred per cent. It may seem strange, but I think my war time experiences specially qualify me for my calling here.'

The colonel gave a little mirthless laugh. 'Ha! Ha! How on earth could that be?' he asked. 'You even said … what was it? That you thought God was dead! You, a man of the church! Incredible!'

Michael saw Macleod straighten his back. A fire came into his eyes.

'I saw hell, Colonel. But I also saw something else. Something unexpected. I saw a selflessness that I had never seen before. It took me through my doubt and showed me that God was there in those trenches. If I could find faith in that hell, I can help others do the same.'

The colonel laughed again. 'And what sort of hell do you think they see in Camberley', he said.

'They may not have experienced the trenches, but they're on their own battlefields. The death of a child, the pain of abandonment, the loss of hope. That's the sort of hell they have to face.'

Even the colonel was briefly silenced by Macleod's strong words.

'Does shell shock stay with you?' asked Michael.

'Yes!' said the colonel. 'That is what I was about to ask.' Michael saw at once the colonel's plan. He wanted to label the vicar, to publicly proclaim his disability.

''It does to some extent' replied Macleod. 'I get terrible headaches, sleeplessness. A sudden noise can startle me.'

'I would never have known. I'm so sorry,' said Michael.

'I try my best to stop it interfering with my life.'

'You have never missed a service since I have known you.' said Michael. 'Even when your wife died.'

'I'm afraid I will have to report the blemish on your service record to the parishioners,' said the colonel.

'If it is a blemish,' said Michael.

'I will be happy to answer any questions from the community,' said Macleod.

'I can't think that there could be any more questions. I'm full of respect for what you have been through,' said Michael.

'You're speaking out of turn,' said the colonel. 'We have a democratic committee, Michael.' He stood up and walked towards the door, followed by the two men. He turned to Macleod before leaving the room. 'Thank you for your candour, Macleod. You will be hearing from us. If you want to contact me about this, you can. It might be easier for all concerned if you just decided to ask the Church authorities for a transfer. Spare a lot of ...'

He was interrupted when the door suddenly opened, narrowly missing his shoulder. A slight, blond woman strode in. She was small, but made up for her diminutive stature with an air of forcefulness. She stood directly in front of the men, barring their exit. It was Macleod's daughter, Hillary. She spoke breathlessly, as if she had been hurrying and she was angry.

'I was told you would be here. I don't like it.' She said.

The colonel was unabashed. 'We're just leaving,' he said.

'I know about your accusations against my father. They're a disgrace,' she continued.

'We all have our jobs to do,' said the colonel.

'It's a shame you can't find better work" said Hillary.

The barb was sharp, particularly because the colonel had found no formal work since his retirement and he was constantly looking for a role to fulfill. Michael thought he saw his face twitch slightly. Macleod broke in to talk to his daughter.

'Don't, dear! It's nothing. I'm sorting it out.' But Hillary was undeterred. This time she turned to Michael.

'Michael, I'm surprised to see you here too.'

Michael tried to be conciliatory. 'It's all right, Hillary. There's no need to worry. We've settled everything.' He felt inadequate and wanted to say more to support Macleod.

Colonel Traverse looked angrily at Michael. He then turned to Hillary. 'I can see this might upset you, but it's in everyone's interest. Don't concern your pretty head about it, young lady. In everyone's interest but not interesting. Ha! Ha! '

Hillary was unabashed. 'It's not in my father's interest, is it? I'd like to know just what grounds you have for stirring up this trouble,' she said.

The colonel straightened his back to tower over the small woman. 'I take exception to that,' he said. 'The matter is confidential and is being handled in the correct manner.'

Macleod tried again to silence his daughter. 'Hillary, dear, I really do not think ...'

'And I hope that you will not come here again on this pretext. Such disloyalty! ' she continued.

The colonel looked pompous. 'You are talking to a former officer of His Majesty's Forces. I will not tolerate charges of disloyalty. Furthermore, I will take whatever steps are necessary to perform my duty.'

'Well, your next step, I suggest, should be out of here,' said Hillary.

'Please, dear,' said Macleod. 'Let us not get angry.'

'Angry, dad! Of course I'm angry!' She turned to Michael. 'Michael, I thought you had more backbone. I know you would never be willingly disloyal to dad.'

The word 'willingly' stung Michael. She was accusing him of unwittingly betraying her father. 'I'm sorry, Hillary,' said Michael. 'I seemed to have achieved the opposite of what I intended in asking for this meeting. Colonel, shall we go now?'

The colonel spoke with a military clip in his voice. The tone by itself was a dressing down. 'Michael I'm not sure what you intended, but the way forward is clear to me. Goodnight vicar. Goodnight, Hillary.'

He pushed roughly past Hillary to walk out of the door. Michael looked at Macleod and Hillary. There was nothing he could find to say. He felt he had let them down. He shrugged. 'I'm sorry,' he said. He then followed the colonel into the cool night air which failed to refresh him. He was angry with himself. Not only had he seemed to be rounding against his friend, but worst of all, it looked like he was Traverse's lackey. It made him despise the colonel and his pompous standards even more than he did before. He wished he had the courage to confront Traverse.

'You've let me down, Rogers. I am not pleased.'

'I felt bound to apologise' said Michael.

'Bound to?' said the colonel. 'Your duty was to support me. We'll talk of this later.'

Michael suddenly felt a rising anger. His response came out of him effortlessly, surprising him. 'No colonel! I'm not taking any further part in this vendetta. In fact, my duty is not to support you but to defend my friend, Macleod.' He felt a deep warmth inside him, as if he had just swallowed a tot of brandy. He knew there would be repercussions but he had spoken his mind.

'You'll hear more about this!', was all the colonel could reply and he stormed off.

CHAPTER 15

I<small>T WAS</small> <small>DIFFICULT</small> for Michael to picture Ruth's face, as he sat at the breakfast table, a newspaper opened at his side. Michael thought the signs were good. The Nazi party was in a civil war. It would self-destruct. He had to talk to Ruth.

Ruth! He could not stop thinking about her, but each time he tried to remember how her dark eyes were matched by her dark brown hair, or how her straight chiselled nose was in proportion to her firm, neatly outlined lips, the memory of her face eluded him. He would have to see her again, so that he could set it in his mind. Besides, he conceded, he longed for the excitement, that nerve-charged feeling of being near her. He also wanted to tell her what happened at Canon Macleod's. He had to admit that he was a little concerned about Colonel Traverse's parting threat, but did not regret saying what he did in the least. He was pleased with himself that he had finally spoken his mind and supported his friend. He knew that it was not going to help his relationship with Sarah, as he knew how close Sarah was to her father. Although somehow it had brought him closer to Ruth.

Suddenly the door bell sounded.

Mrs Waller went to see who was calling, bothered by being called away from rolling her pastry. She hurried to the door, muttering to herself, and putting flour all over her gray hair, as she tried to brush back the loose strands. Michael smiled as he heard her favorite exclamation.

'No peace for the wicked!'

He strained to hear voices, holding his cup halfway to his mouth. He heard a woman's footsteps, advancing confidently, and the door swung open.

It was the wrong woman. When he saw Sarah, Michael realized in an instant how much he longed to see Ruth. Sarah had tried to look elegant and was sporting an unfashionably broad-brimmed hat, which sat too far back on her head so that it evoked the peasant rather than the pastoral chic intended.

'Michael, I swear you've been hiding. I would be offended if I didn't know of your devotion! What has happened between you and Daddy? He doesn't seem very happy with you. He said something about not wanting me to see you again! We have to sit down and talk. You're going soon, and we haven't even discussed my trip to India. We haven't chosen the ring. Now…'

Michael decided to beat Sarah at her own game, and was equally peremptory as he stood up, his sudden movement interrupting her. He took a hasty gulp of tea, and looked at his watch. It was a fair imitation of a man with a train to catch.

'Oh my gosh! Is that really the time? Sarah, I'm late already. Very sorry! Must go!'

He did not know where he had found a sudden talent for acting. Perhaps his mother's tastes were rubbing off on him. His plan had arrived, fully-formed, in his mind the moment Sarah had strode in. He put his hand amicably on her shoulder. 'Do excuse me, Sarah! I'll catch up with you later.' As he left, he called over his shoulder. 'Mrs Waller will fetch you some tea, and mum will be down in an instant. Cheerio!'

He snatched a hat from the stand in the hallway and lunged out of the door, without glancing backwards to see Sarah's reaction. It was enough to feel her eyes, it seemed to him, boring into his back.

Michael found himself facing another door, feeling furtive. It was Ruth's. He hoped she would open it, so sparing him any awkward explanations. He was not expecting the looming figure that seemed to bar his entrance. It was that of a tall good-looking young man, slim, yet athletic. He was in tennis whites, but his expression was not sporting. He looked at Michael quizzically, and with irritation.

'Yes?'

The tone was accusing.

'Is Ruth there?'

'Ruth, it's for you' he said loudly, not even turning his head and looking as if a bad smell under his nose had just got worse.

This must be the young man his mother had talked about. The one who was thought to be a suitable match for Ruth – affluent, ambitious, from an eminent Jewish family.

Michael was glad to see Ruth in the gloom of the hallway, not yet in her tennis whites, if indeed the plan was for her to play with the young man.

Suddenly Ben appeared at his mother's side, and broke the tension. 'Michael! It's awfully good to see you. Have you brought Toby?'

'No, Ben. He's busy digging up my mother's flowers in the garden. How's your bowling practice doing? Do you think you'll manage to get on the cricket team? Have you mastered over-arm bowling, yet?'

'I'll need some help, I think'.

'Am I in your way?' said the young man, not moving and unable to disguise sarcasm in his voice. There was something zoological in his guarding Ruth's home, thought Michael, like a bird puffing out its chest to intimidate a rival on its patch.

Ruth appeared on the now crowded threshold.

Michael spoke quickly. 'There you are, Ruth! I thought you'd forgotten.'

It was a gamble, and not very straight, but Michael had an idea that he thought might work. His own duplicity and determination took him by surprise but they were unstoppable.

Ruth froze for a moment, with a look of utter perplexity.

'You know!' he continued. 'Our rendezvous with my aunt to assess that Dresden china she wants to sell. She's been counting on your advice.' He was relieved to see that Ruth had also found some acting skill from somewhere, and there seemed to be a meeting of minds and wishes.

'Yes. Stupid of me! What a muddle I've made of everything. Gabriel, I'm sorry. Our game will have to wait till later. The Smiths will let us use their court another time.'

Gabriel's hand fell away heavily from the threshold with a movement of pique.

'Sorry! Hope this isn't a bore for you,' said Michael.

Gabriel looked skywards.

Ruth spoke to the young man. 'I do apologize, Gabriel. Let me just grab my hat and bag.'

Michael suddenly saw Ben looking at him forlornly. He saw himself as a boy of Ben's age, standing near a front door. It was the door of his boarding school and he was dressed in his school uniform, waiting for his parents to take him out for Sunday tea. He saw the daunting figure of matron looming over him, the gray hair scraped severely back into a bun. She looked uncharacteristically benign, as she peered down at him. 'I'm sorry, dear,' she had said. 'Your parents just telephoned and they can not come today.'

Michael spoke quickly.

'Ben, come too!'

Ruth looked at Michael questioningly but quickly grasped her son's hand.

'No time to lose!' Michael continued with his rapid-fire speech. He did not want Gabriel to get a word in edgeways and he was fearful that Ruth's grandmother would appear with awkward questions.

'Pile into the car,' he continued. 'Good to meet you, Gabriel. Hope we'll have more time, soon.'

Gabriel looked at him and said, 'It's lucky I don't like Dresden china.'

As the car turned on the gravel, Ruth looked flustered for the first time.' Michael, what are we doing?'

'I thought a day trip to London on the train would be fun,' said Michael. 'Ben, are you good at keeping things under your hat. This is to be a secret trip, because Gabriel could not come with us. Ruth, do you think we have time to go to London. We could go and see Buckingham Palace?'

Ruth shook her head in disbelief. 'I don't know why I'm doing this. You're making a dishonest woman out of me.' Their eyes met, and they both laughed.

Michael then grew serious.

'Did you see the papers, Ruth? The Nazi party is in total disarray.,'

Ruth's lighthearted expression disappeared.

'No, Michael. Hitler has just become stronger. This massacre is just the beginning. It shows how much he wants power, total control. And you think he's going to stop there?'

'So it's going to get worse?'

'I saw the other story in the newspaper. It said Hitler demands blind obedience, unquestioning loyalty from his troops. His troops. Not Germany's, not the government's. His troops. And you know what happens when people no longer question their loyalties? They become like animals.'

An anxious small voice came from the back of the car. 'What is it, Mutti? What's the matter?'

Ruth turned to smile at her son.

'It's nothing, liebschon. We're going to see the King's house.'

They only just managed to buy the tickets before the 10.47 pulled alongside the platform. Ben was so exuberant, he jumped up and down.

Suddenly someone tapped Michael on the shoulder, and he saw Ruth's eyes widen in alarm.

'Michael, what on earth are you doing here?'

He spun round to see his aunt Estelle.

Michael stammered in alarm. 'We're just boarding this train to London, aunt.' He sounded stupid.

'Well. I can see that, dear,' she replied. She looked questioningly at Ruth and Ben.

'We're going to see the guards at Buckingham Palace,' said Ben.

They all climbed in to the same carriage and sat down heavily on the velvety upholstery.

The secret was out. Embarrassment and explanation would follow. It was useless to ask Estelle to keep quiet about their meeting. A physical impossibility – like trying to prevent an echo from resounding in a valley.

Estelle, though, was smiling. The narrow brim of her hat supported a surplus of brightly colored silk flowers. Absurdly, the fox fur, her hallmark accessory, was still draped over her shoulders; the beady eyes of the animal's head seemed to follow the direction of her gaze.

'What a lovely day!' she said.

There was no question from her, no surprise registering on her face. Some inner thought was making her cheerful. 'Buckingham Palace! I went up there as a girl. It was not the guards that fascinated me – that came later, with the dances and the romances.' She chuckled, at the word 'romances' and gave Michael a meaningful look he was at a loss to interpret.

'No, Ben,' she continued, 'It was the horses that interested me. Beautiful animals, with gleaming coats and shining brass tack. I always wanted a horse.'

Estelle could not stop talking. She hardly stopped for breath. It was as if she were trying to shield her companions' embarrassment, thought Michael.

'I'm on my way to Liberty's. You know the store, of course. It looks like a Tudor building, just by Regent's Street. I love dressmaking and nothing beats a Liberty print. I'm meeting my friend Beatrice for lunch. She's a widow, too. It's not easy to be on your own.'

Here she stopped and looked for agreement from Ruth, who just nodded solemnly.

'I had a wonderful life with my husband, Terence.' Estelle's eyes started to well up. 'Of course we didn't have children.'

She searched in her bag for a handkerchief and dabbed her eyes. She willed a brave smile and then suddenly patted Ben on the knees. Ben had been looking out of the window, and was so startled by Estelle's precipitate gesture that he jumped.

'I want you to have this, Ben,' she said.

A shiny half crown was pressed into his palm. She had won a friend. 'Thanks ever so much!'

Finally there was silence except for the sound of the rhythmic rattling of the train over the rails. Estelle sat back in her seat, her rounded figure, rocked gently by the train, and her brimful of flowers nodding gently. She gazed out of the window, smiling once more, to herself.

It was Michael's turn to smooth over the unspoken questions with talk. 'I thought that we'd catch a bus to Lyon's Corner House to have lunch, after seeing the Palace. We can go the park afterwards, and perhaps hire a rowing boat.'

Michael thought Ruth was being too quiet, and was concerned that she felt uncomfortable meeting his aunt under these circumstances. Her hands were resting in her lap, and, without speaking, he grasped her hand and squeezed it gently. Estelle leaned further towards the window in renewed concentration of the scene outside. She was interrupted by her nephew.

'Aunt, I think I should tell you that Ruth is helping you to price your Dresden china today.'

'Yes?' Estelle asked, mildly. 'I see.'

When the train pulled in to Victoria station, with its cathedral-like dimensions and vaulted glass ceiling, all self-consciousness had disappeared.

'I've been meaning to go to Liberty's myself,' said Ruth.

'Come with me, my dear,' said Estelle. 'Michael can take Ben to see the guards at the Palace and you can meet him for lunch. I'll put you in a taxi, myself.'

Ruth looked at Michael for his agreement. Michael spoke to Ben.

'Why not? Ben, that's all right, isn't it? Liberty's is not for us. We'll meet you in the café at two o'clock.'

Ben looked suspicious, but after Ruth whispered in his ear he seemed resigned to the scheme.

She's probably offered him a little bribe, thought Michael.

Michael was disappointed that Ruth could leave him so easily, but there was a bonus. His aunt was in league with her, and that acceptance by a member of his family gladdened him. The two women walked off briskly, and as Ruth turned to wave to them he was suddenly reminded of the farewells he would have to make in a couple of weeks, when he would leave for India from a similar London station, with its grimy skylights and constant crowds.

People hurried past him and the boy, with their suitcases, and bags and he felt unsettled, as if he were a refugee. For the first time, the army was no longer an anchor for him, yet neither was he at home in England. He had the same sense of foreboding that he had felt in the cinema with Ruth when he had seen the newsreel about the Austrian Chancellor. The old order was falling away. Europe would dissolve into chaos, India would become ungovernable, and the message of that strange Indian lawyer, Gandhi, in his dhoti, would embolden the population to revolt against the British. He looked down at Ben, who was watching him silently, waiting for him to move. He did not know whether to hold the boy's hand, but decided against it.

They passed the newsagent's stand and the headlines glared out from the Daily Mail. 'Berlin in Hitler's Iron Grip. Mobs on Rampage'. He edged closer to read more, and a tall suited man jostled him as he crossed his gaze. It was enough to break Michael's concentration and he looked round for Ben. He was not there. Frantically he turned a full circle. Still no sign of the boy. He raced forward, thinking that perhaps he had tried to follow his mother, but as he approached the exit, he saw only adults hurrying back and forth. His mind raced. Where could the boy have gone? He was too young to be on his own. Terrible scenarios crossed his mind- the boy running into traffic, or standing in wide-eyed terror, prey to a Fagin-like figure of the criminal world. He thought of Ruth's despair if the boy were really lost.

He ran back to the newsagent, hoping to see the small figure, with the spindly legs encased in those long gray socks. Nothing. The only movement beneath the towering adults was a small dachshund on a leash, attached to the hand of a stout lady with a voluminous bosom, lace floating from her bodice like the wake on the prow of a boat. This silly image jarred with Michael's alarmed state of mind.

'Ben, Ben, where are you?' He found himself calling the boy, and people looked at him, disapproving of the volume of his voice.

'Can I help you?' A calm, thin voice seemed to come from the direction of his elbow. He saw a small, wiry woman of about sixty, in a brown hat and a shapeless, maroon dress that hung limply on her bony frame.

'I've lost a boy. I can't think what's happened to him.'

By now someone else had stopped, as elderly gentleman in round, horn-rimmed spectacles.

'What did he look like?'

Michael was looking in all directions, over the crowd's shoulders.

'Eight years old. Dark hair. White shirt. Gray shorts. '

His mind was racing. Should he fetch a policeman, a railway official?

The help should have been welcomingly sympathetic, but it distracted him, and he became more agitated.

'I don't know how he could have disappeared. He was just here.'

The newspaper seemed so unimportant, now. The world had shrunk to the all-absorbing anxiety of losing a child.

'Now where, dear?' said the thin lady. 'You'll have to tell us more.'

Michael's collar felt very hot and he spoke without thinking.

'He wouldn't have run away. He can't have gone far.'

Suddenly he saw the back of a small figure in gray shorts and white shirt. He felt a wave of relief and ran forward. The boy was holding someone's hand. A smartly dressed middle aged woman was leading the child. He approached her and as he drew level with them, the woman shot him a glance of firm rebuke for getting too close. The boy was not Ben.

Anger swelled up in Michael. What did the child think he was doing? He would give him a very stern rebuke when he found him. When he found him? Doubt of ever doing so surged through him. He then felt great pity for Ben. The boy must be so distressed. He redoubled his search efforts, craning his neck to look over the crowds. The woman in the maroon dress was blocking his way.

'You'll have to show me exactly where you were dear.'

She would have been irritating, but Michael needed whatever help he could find.

'My boy got lost once,' said the bespectacled gent, unhelpfully. 'Dreadful business. Found him in the men's cloakroom after a couple of hours.'

The lavatories. Michael looked for the sign. They were nearby and he ran over, tripping over people's feet with a perfunctory "Excuse me!"

The cloakrooms revealed no child, only some stern-looking men, suspicious of such an abrupt intrusion of their privacy.

It was time to find a policeman.

'Here I am, a battle-hardened soldier, and I go to pieces when a child wanders off,' thought Michael.'How could I have been so stupid?'

In the distance he saw a black uniform. It was a police man. He had someone by the hand – a small person, a boy. It was Ben. Michael sighed audibly. His panic evaporated in an instant, and he would no longer acknowledge it. He thought he had behaved perfectly rationally, and had always thought the boy was just out of sight. Yet as he congratulated himself, he saw Ben's face. The boy's head was bent, in shadow, but the grimy streaks of tears were not to be disguised. Small sobs lifted his shoulders intermittently. Michael felt a wave of compassion. Without thinking he rushed forward and crouched down to embrace the child. Ben, unabashed, put his head on Michael's shoulder so that his shirt soon felt damp. His muffled voice was barely audible.

'I was following you, but it wasn't you! It was someone else. He had the same clothes.'

'You've found your son, then, sir!' said the police officer.

Michael did not correct him. He liked being mistaken for Ben's father. It made him feel proud, and for the first time he imagined he could fulfill the role. He muttered an apology and held Ben firmly by the hand. Again he passed the newsstand. The same headlines were penned on the board in front of the stacks newspapers. Sales were brisk as the vendor handed out copies. But Michael was indifferent to the news now. He could only think that Ben was safe. Priorities had shifted.

CHAPTER 16

Lyon's Corner House was crowded and noisy. Not even a piano, play-ing a medley of popular music, could drown out the voices. The wait-resses in black-and-white uniforms were weaving through the customers seated at the small round tables, decked in white cloths. They balanced silver trays loaded with plates, cups and tea pots. These women were so renowned that they had their own name – 'nippies'. Michael smiled at the memory of poor Mrs Waller, trying to balance a rattling tray of tea cups at the garden party, and pictured her as a sort of rogue waitress in this restaurant, causing consternation among the customers as her tray wobbled perilously over their heads.

Most of the customers were women, both young and middle-aged, dressed smartly in their London outfits, with a variety of fashionable hats, sitting atop neatly coiffed hair. Some were joined by men in suits. Marble-clad pillars ran the length of the large room, and were topped by leaf-shaped glass shades, that threw upwards a muted, golden light to the ceiling, supplementing the meager daylight from a far window. There were not many children. A young girl of about six was sitting primly with an older woman, probably her grandmother, in a blue dress, sipping juice.

Ben was entranced. He looked all about the room as they made their way to the table. There was no sign of his earlier sadness, and Michael and he had an instinctive, unspoken agreement not to tell his mother of the incident. She only noticed signs of a close friendship developing between Michael and the boy. She saw the way Ben looked at his mentor as if to take cues from his behavior, the way he stood close to him, and smiled at jokes they shared.

'My goodness, Ruth, how many shopping bags do you have there? When am I going to see those dresses on you? Let me take a peek.'

'No, really, they're nothing special. Your aunt persuaded me to buy them. She was so kind. She said she had always bought her dresses and fabrics at Liberty's. She said I reminded her of when she was young, just before she married Terence.'

'I suppose you could not stop her talking. I hope she didn't get all weepy talking about her husband.'

'No, but she said something I didn't understand.'

'What was that?' asked Michael.

'She told me that she understood and that I was not to be afraid. Do you think she was talking about Germany?'

Michael knew immediately that she was talking about Ruth and himself, and that, as an inveterate sentimentalist, she now championed their liaison, but he could not tell her.

'It's unusual for her to be so cryptic,' was all he could say.

'I have something that you can see, though,' said Ruth. She searched through one of the bags and gave Michael a small package wrapped in tissue paper. Michael was puzzled and flattered that she had bought him something. Silently he unwrapped it. It was a gleaming green silk tie, with a delicate pattern woven into it. He was not surprised that Ruth had made such a good choice.

'Thank you Ruth.' His tone became teasing and he looked into her eyes. 'Green. The color of spring, of young love.' He paused. 'Of hope!'

Ruth looked at him quizzically until Ben interrupted her thoughts.

'Don't I get something, Mutti?' he asked.

'You know you do!' said his mother. 'I went to that big toy shop next to Liberty's and this is for you.' She handed him a small paper bag.

Michael joined Ruth in giving the boy all their attention as he grabbed the contents of the package. It was a wind-up train, painted in red and black. He immediately put it on the floor to see it speed off towards the next table. A stern young man, finding the toy at his feet, frowned as he returned it to Ben. He looked severely at the presumed parents. For the second time that day, Michael felt happy to be mistaken for the boy's father.

The waitress interrupted them to take their order. When she left, it was Ben who broke the silence of the two adults.

'Mother's going somewhere special tomorrow night.' Ruth tried to hide her embarrassment by looking distractedly at the other diners.

'Where's that?' asked Michael.

'O, it's really nothing. Just a little dinner.' Ruth wanted to sound casual, but she was being evasive.

'She's going with Gabriel' said Ben, unaware of the effect of his news.

Michael looked at Ruth. He was indignant, but he tried, like Ruth to appear unconcerned. 'With Gabriel? Why is that?' he asked.

Ruth was agitated. She was looking urgently in her handbag for something.

'Is it some sort of special celebration, Ruth?' Michael was trying to keep the sarcasm out of his voice.

'No. It was something that was arranged a long time ago. A small country restaurant. Nothing special,' she said.

Ben spoke up. 'It's that nice hotel on the London road, grandmamma said.' He was oblivious to the effect his words had on Michael.

Michael could not hide the hostility in his voice, 'Ah, a hotel! You seem to be visiting a number of hotels lately!' he said.

'Really, Michael! It's just a dinner. He's an old friend.' Ruth glanced at her son to see how he was reacting to their voices, which were too animated for her liking.

Ben was finishing his orange juice noisily with a straw, happily kicking his legs back and forth with childish insouciance.

'Is there anybody else going with you?' Michael asked.

'Why is that important? Let's not talk any more of this nonsense, Michael' Ruth looked intently into his eyes, in an effort to reassure him. Such a look would normally have pleased him, but now it gave him more anguish.

'Of course, it's none of my business who you go out to dinner with!' He felt her hand reach his under the table and he took his away, peevishly. He tried to resist speaking any more about her dinner with Gabriel, but it was no use. 'Perhaps you'd like to take me along?' he said.

'Here is our food' said Ruth, ending the conversation abruptly.

Michael was lost in thought. He could neither continue to reproach her, nor could he carry on a normal conversation. He turned to Ben. 'That chop looks good. I hope you're saving room for desert. Where's my coffee. Didn't I order it when we first arrived? What has happened to the service here?'

Michael's anger came spilling out with his words. Yet it was not anger that he was feeling. It was sadness. A crowd of dismal images jostled for his attention – waiting to board the boat train for India, his mother's stoical expression at his father's funeral, in spite of her inner devastation, Ben standing on his matchstick legs in a crowd of strangers, his face streaked with tears, his father's empty shoes left in the cupboard upstairs.

Suddenly he wanted to leave; he needed to be by himself. He was torturing himself. How could he have imagined a lasting relationship with Ruth, with Ben? He was engaged to Sarah. 'Anyway,' he thought, 'her family would never accept a Christian marriage. My career will be in tatters if I marry a Jewish woman, and one with a questionable past.' The regiment was more enlightened than before the Great War, but social expectations were still very high.

What was he doing? Why was he even thinking remotely about marriage to Ruth? He would have to return to India in ten short days. It would be a long time until he would return to England – a year and a half, at least. He would be taking his leave in the hilltop resorts or in Srinagar. Then there was Vera and Sarah.

He stood up before he had made a conscious decision to do so. He stammered slightly as he spoke. 'This is a little abrupt, I know, and I... I hope you don't mind, but I have to go to my outfitters... to Gieves, to get a dinner jacket. I hope you don't mind if I just leave the money for lunch and for a taxi. I'll go home separately.'

'Michael is there something wrong?' asked Ruth

Michael's voice was hollow. 'Nothing.!' 'I just thought, while I was here ... it's not long before I have to go back to India, as you know. I do have a few errands. I hope you have fun at your hotel dinner.' He wished he had not said that. It sounded so peevish. Ben looked up at him, unaware of the tension.

'I'll see you back at home, then,' said Ruth.

'Oh, I expect so.' He tried to sound unconcerned. It was rude of him to leave them, but he could no longer stay. He felt like sitting down again, of grabbing Ruth by the hand, of kissing her on the cheek, of ordering some huge, extravagant desert for Ben. Instead he weaved his way between the tables and out of the room to the busy indifference of the London street. Men in bowler hats and Fedoras pushed past him and women dawdled with friends and children. Bright red and white double decker buses toiled noisily along the roadway with the black cabs and klaxoning cars. Michael walked quickly, spurred by the pressure of what brief time was left to him in England. He thought how little would change between the present and the day of his embarkation. He thought there had been enough turbulence on this short leave. Yet he sensed there was a lot more to come.

CHAPTER 17

'HELLO! IS THERE ANYONE at home?'

Estelle had arrived unannounced. Michael was in the kitchen, preparing coffee.

'I'm here aunt.'

She bustled into the room, clutching a shopping basket. 'Good morning, darling!'

Michael felt like a schoolboy, when she addressed him like that, but he realized, at the same time, that he was her surrogate child, a compensation for her own childless marriage.

'Heavens! That coffee smells good! Do pour me a cup, please. Where is your mother?'

'She'll be back later. She went to London.'

'Ah!' Estelle seemed satisfied at this news but somehow she did not seem surprised. Michael guessed that she had wanted to find him alone.

She sat down heavily, looking larger than usual in a décolleté dress that emphasized her expansive bosom. She looked searchingly at Michael, and he guessed she was about to launch on the real purpose of her visit. She started talking in a tentative way.

'You're going back to India soon. We'll miss you.'

'You'll look after mum, won't you?'

'She'll be fine. But what about you? You'll be missing someone you may not have an opportunity to see again for a long time.'

'What are you driving at aunt?'

'I saw you, Michael. I saw her. You could not have disguised those looks between you in the train, Michael. I've never seen you like that before with any girl. You're in love with Ruth, aren't you?'

Michael bristled. 'Even if I felt certain feelings for her – there are too many barriers for us to form an attachment. Surely you can see that. She's Jewish, she has a past, and she has a child and her family are arranging for her to marry a suitable Jewish man. I could never combine my career with those obstacles. Only recently, a colonel in the regiment wanted to marry a divorcée and he is being forced to resign his commission.'

'It seems to me you have given it a lot of thought,' said Estelle.

'It's just too difficult. There's no need for thought.'

There was a long pause. Michael was feeling resentful and sipped some coffee nervously. 'Why does Estelle have to bring up all these questions?' he thought. 'Why can't she just be her old, diverting self?'

He was still smarting from the revelation that Ruth was going out to dinner with Gabriel. What would happen when Michael left for India? Gabriel would loose no time. He has the family's consent and he and Ruth would be married in a few months. How could Ruth let Gabriel into her house when she hardly knew him? But maybe she has known him for some time. How could Ruth do this to him? She couldn't feel very deeply for him.

Estelle sat up very straight. Her usual affable expression had changed. She was serious, her eyes focused unrelentingly on her nephew.

'I've seen it all,' she continued. 'I've seen a generation of young men who yearned for the chance to live. They went off to war, the Great War, and they never came back. I've seen their mothers, their loved ones, struggling to find sense in a life without them. And then I've seen people who have thrown happiness away, because they thought there was always a tomorrow, always a second chance. Many were waiting for the perfect person, the perfect moment.' She shook her head dolefully. 'They're my age now, and they're still waiting. They wonder bitterly why they weren't lucky. They can not admit it was they who made their own luck.' Estelle let her words sink in before continuing. Her small plump hand reach across to Michael's. 'Sometimes fate takes our happiness away. That is tragic, and I should know. But do you know what is worse? It's when the chance to love and be loved is tossed away. That is what you are doing, Michael.'

Michael was dismissive. 'You don't understand Estelle. I have to go away for nearly two years. I can't ditch my career. Ruth's family wants her to marry a Jewish man. My mother wants me to marry Sarah and

Sarah is coming out to India next year. That's what fate is bringing me.'

'Now you're being flippant,' said Estelle. 'I've seen you with Sarah, Michael, and I've seen you with Ruth. Even a fool would see that you have no love for Sarah.'

'How would you know what I feel, aunt? It's true that I enjoy Ruth's company. I even seek it out, sometimes. I find her attractive, very attractive. Who wouldn't? And I worry about her, away from her parents, having to run away from Germany with her son, harbouring terrible memories of her time there recently. Like everyone else, darn it, I feel sorry for her.' Estelle sat silently, unmoved by his defence. Michael felt compelled to continue. 'But it's not just that! I find her fun to be with. She makes me happy. She's a diversion while I'm here on leave.'

'A diversion! Listen to yourself, Michael!' said Estelle. 'She makes you happy, you feel compassion for her, you want to be with her all the time, you look for her when she's not with you. Can't you hear yourself? You love her. You can't deny it.'

'Love! I don't know. Love hardly comes into it. I have my life to live, my career to build. What would I be without a career? I would be no use to myself or anyone else.'

Estelle was unruffled by Michael's protestations. 'You would always find a goal and find work outside the army,' she said. 'You underestimate yourself, Michael. You were always enterprising. Remember when you worked for the local paper just before you went to Sandhurst? They offered you a good position. You could easily find a job in the City. Finding work is far easier than finding a true partner. That chance may come just once in a lifetime.'

'It's fine for you to say that, but what about Ruth? It's clear she doesn't love me. Even if I did love her, I can't spend my time in India pining for someone who is willing to trade me for her grandmother's choice at the drop of a hat.'

'So that's what's eating at you!' said Estelle. 'Michael can't you see that Ruth loves you too? Just as I saw it in your eyes, I saw it in hers too. Remember that Ruth has been through a lot. Try to see it from her point of view. She sees you are engaged to Sarah, going away for a long time and that Sarah is coming to visit you. She needs a secure future for her little boy. She sees that her grandmother can at least give her this. I know you are the one she loves, but you have to show her. You have to give her both love and security.'

'Sometimes I wish I could just have a marriage arranged, like they do in India.'

Estelle was irritated. 'I'm just telling you not to be a fool, Michael. Don't be one of those old people left behind because their heads over-ruled their hearts. You have to break off your engagement to Sarah, but don't dare tell Gladys that I told you. '

'I can't stay now. But please, think about what I have said. Tell your mother I'll telephone her later.'

CHAPTER 18

THE NEXT MORNING Michael was just picking up the newspaper at the breakfast table, when he heard the telephone ring. He wondered, stupidly, if it was Ruth. Then he heard his mother talk in hushed tones. He wondered what little drama was occurring in the neighbourhood today. A cancellation of the amateur dramatics meeting? That yappy little dog down the road getting lost again? He hoped, malevolently, that it had taken off once and for all, into the sunset. Or maybe it was his aunt, telling his mother about his trip to London with Ruth. Impossible! Estelle would have called her last night, as soon as she had dumped her shopping over the threshold and before she could kick off her pinching shoes, or put the kettle on for tea.

He sat down for breakfast, but before he could read the headlines his mother sidled in. She had been looking sad every morning for the past week, knowing that his leave was coming to an end. She had kept doing little things to please him lately, such as making his favorite meal or buying him a leather photograph frame with a picture of his father and herself in it - the sort of frame that would travel easily, even on campaign. Yet when she came in this time, she looked even more uneasy and very solemn. It worried him.

'Has something happened?' he asked.

'I'm afraid it has' she said.

'It has nothing to do with Ruth?' His anxiety made him lose his inhibition.

'No, dear, it's someone else.'

'Not Estelle?'

All the irritation his aunt usually elicited in him vanished and was replaced by anxiety for her.

'No, it's Reverend Macleod.'

Momentary relief suddenly gave way to renewed concern.

'What happened? Tell me.'

'He was in his car last night, traveling towards Godalming. The car struck a tree. Michael...' she paused and looked anxiously at him, '... he's dead.'

He could not take the news in, at first. Canon Macleod, his mentor, his friend, the one person who could put him totally at ease, who would listen to him, console him, who seemed to have an innate wisdom. Now he was gone. He thought of his daughters.

Gladys sat down beside Michael in silence and put a consoling hand on his arm. Michael sat in silence his thoughts racing.

They had killed him. He recalled the voice of colonel Traverse, and the terrible irony of his words, 'Let us take all emotion out of this, shall we?'

There was no longer anything Michael could do in the face of these bullies, for that is what he judged Traverse and his supporters to be. Canon Macleod had died while his reputation was being dragged through the mud. He deserved better, his family deserved better.

He suddenly thought of what he could do to help. He would go to the vicarage to speak to Macleod's daughter Hillary. She must be there now, making arrangements for the funeral, and helping to sort out parish business.

There was a feeling that took him by surprise. In his sorrow, he wanted to talk to Ruth. She would understand his grief; she had had her share of suffering. Yet how could he visit her? Gabriel could still be staying at her house, making the situation awkward. Besides, he had been so abrupt in leaving Ruth and Ben at the café, that he would be the last person Ruth wanted to see.

The telephone rang in the hallway and Gladys went to answer it. For the second time that morning, Michael hoped it was Ruth.

'It's for you, dear,' his mother called.

His hopes were raised. He heard the familiar voice of a young woman on the other end.

'Michael! It's Sarah. We've just heard the news. What a terrible business!'

She was talking fast, not allowing any comment from Michael.

'Daddy, of course, is very sad about it. He said it was a great shame, but that in a way it solved the problem about the parish.'

'How can you say such a thing at this time?' said Michael.

'Well, I'm sorry.' She sounded sulky. 'But it's only the truth. But let bygones be bygones. I'll be at the funeral tomorrow with mum and dad, and I'll see you there.'

'Yes, I'll be there.'

'And afterwards,' she continued, 'let's do something. We haven't been seeing enough of each other lately, and before you know it, you'll be off.'

'We'll talk about that later. Goodbye.'

'Cheerio Michael! And don't be upset about this. I know you get a bit gloomy sometimes.'

Michael felt irritated at her levity as he put the receiver down heavily on its cradle. He knew he had to break off the engagement. He was going to have to find the right time.

There were many cars parked in the wide gravel driveway in front of the vicarage. The front door was open and a middle-aged gentleman that Michael recognized from church was standing just inside.

'You're Michael. Hillary's in the drawing room, you can just go in.'

Hillary was sitting, shoulders hunched on the sofa. An elderly gray-haired woman – an aunt thought Michael – was sitting next to her with her hand on her arm. Hillary managed a weak smile as she looked up at him.

'Thank you for coming, Michael. Please sit down. Don't worry. I'm all right.'

She was holding a small battered book in her hands and she saw Michael looking at it.

'It's stupid. Do you know what this is? He gave me this just before he left. It's a prayer book he carried with him for years and years. He said that eventually just the feel of the leather covers were a comfort to him. It was his talisman.'

Michael stared at her.

'Don't worry. I know what you're thinking. He didn't harm himself. He gave it to me on the spur of the moment. It was because I was upset. My daughter Daisy had just been prescribed some strong medicine, because she was not doing so well. She has been having epileptic fits, so he was trying to comfort me. He was quite cheerful when he left. He had another reason to be optimistic. He had been helping the government and so he had a sense of mission quite separate from his religious calling.'

Michael looked at Hillary with curiosity.

'I'm not quite sure of the details,' she continued, 'but he was giving them intelligence about Germany that he gleaned from the community or wherever he could find it. That was why he met with that young German neighbour, Ruth. She was giving him information about Germany.' Michael felt a surge of interest. He also felt a curious pride in Ruth, a vindication of his admiration for her. He suddenly realized why Ruth was in Macleod's house when he had met her on that rainy morning and he understood her bond with Macleod now. They had been united in their resistance against the Nazis.

'You see,' said Hillary, 'he served his country to the end. When you think of what those sanctimonious old fools were pinning on him, it's ironic, isn't it?'

Michael nodded.

'I have a strange feeling he had a premonition of his death,' said Hillary.

'Why do you say that?'

'It was the way he looked at me when he left. The way ...' she looked down and her lip started to tremble...the way he kissed me on the forehead as he went out. It was unusual.'

Michael thought of the foreboding about his own safety when his mother and the Fairbrothers had warned him.

Hillary brightened. 'Anyway, he would never have despaired. Those wretched men could not have destroyed his spirit. Not even the Great War could do that.

'They're coming to the funeral tomorrow.'

Michael raised his eyebrows slightly.

'It's alright.' said Hillary. 'I have a surprise for them. It will be a memorial service they won't forget in a hurry. A service no one will forget.'

CHAPTER 19

THE ORGAN WAS PLAYING softly as Michael entered the church with his mother. All the pews were full as he walked down the aisle. Suddenly he saw someone he had not expected to see. Ruth was sitting discreetly at the end of a pew at the side of the church. She was alone, dressed in a dark jacket and a black hat with a small veil shielding her eyes. He hoped she would see him, but she was looking down. He saw Sarah, sitting towards the front of the church, next to her parents. Her father was reading the order of service, wishing to follow protocol to the last, thought Michael. Sarah smiled and waved. She looked inappropriately jovial.

Hillary was sitting in the front pew, next to her daughter Daisy and her relatives. Michael wondered what she had meant by the surprise she had for her father's detractors. She was not one to exaggerate and he sensed she had something shocking to tell the community.

The coffin was carried by a group of men Michael did not recognize, acting as pall bearers. He noticed one elderly man in army uniform, with a string of medals on his chest.

The service was calm, at first; starting with the hymn 'The Lord is my Shepherd'. The elderly priest began the service, but his words were muffled by the sound of Daisy, crying next to her mother. It was a strange, moaning sound, as if she were trying to say, 'No, no!' She was led out, down the centre aisle by an elderly female relative, staggering with her awkward gait, her face wet, and her eyes wide.

Hillary advanced to the lectern to give her address, and all coughing and fidgeting stopped. Everyone looked at the elegant woman facing them, dressed in a tailored black dress, her face unexpectedly calm. Michael saw that she was still clutching the small leather prayer book her father had given her. She had no notes, and paused for a moment to look at the congregation, with a hint of defiance in her eyes.

'You are all mourning my father with me. He would have been honoured at such a turn out. I know all of you have memories of him, and many of you have shared them with me recently. But you did not fully know my dad.' She paused and took a deep breath. 'I want to give you a small picture of the man I knew and loved. Some of you will be surprised, even shocked, by what I have to say.'

Hillary now had the silent attention of the whole congregation.

'This is a day I have been dreading all my life. The day the world would seem emptier. The day that, no matter how old I was, I would be left an orphan.'

Michael noticed a few women around him dabbing their eyes with the corners of their handkerchiefs.

Her voice grew tremulous.

'The day I could never find my father, no matter how many faces I scanned in the crowds, nor how many corners of the earth I probed. He is gone, and I can never tell him how much I loved him.'

Hillary straightened her back, and looked boldly at the congregation, shifting her gaze from one side of the church to the other, as if gathering them all, with that one look, to concentrate on her words. Her voice became more confident.

'Why, then, is it that I feel so strangely at ease? It is because he is not really gone. The unswerving love that he gave to his family and to all of us changed us forever. He helped put this chaotic world into focus – not just by his preaching. That was part of it, I know. But by his faith in us, by the joy he took in just being with each of us. It worked like a contagion we couldn't help catching.

Dad was not perfect. He would be the first one admit his faults. He would get very gloomy at times, irrationally so. He would often become teary-eyed, to the embarrassment of many around him. When dad was giving the funerary address of old Mrs Evans, someone he had known for years, he was seen to wipe the tears away with the back of his hand. In the end the bereaved found themselves putting their arms around dad to comfort him. At weddings, it is the mother of the bride who is supposed to cry. When dad officiated people could be in for a surprise. He was often the one with tears in his eyes.'

There was quiet laughter from the congregation.

'You see,' said Hillary, 'he would probably have known the bride since she was a young girl, and followed her life through to her wedding day. Such emotions were endearing to some of us. It made others uncomfortable. This brings me to something else? His experience of the Great War.'

There were stirrings of discomfort in the Church.

'I know that he was vilified as being a coward, a man who shunned the front, faking a mental crisis. Others stayed on, his accusers said, to face death and horror. He abandoned them.

'In fact he had shell shock, from which he never truly recovered. He would start at sudden noises; he would withdraw for hours at a time, and have terrible headaches. It was God, he said, who helped him through. The image of the crucifixion gave him the strength to face the agonies he saw as he relived the terror of those French battlefields.

'Strange, isn't it, how many of his accusers stayed safely behind the lines? Look at their histories! Look at them! How many of them had to witness the horrors that my dad saw?'

Michael saw Hillary look directly at Colonel Traverse who coughed loudly.

'Do I sound angry? '

Heads now turned to follow her gaze and there were mutterings as people recognised its target.

'Yes! I am angry. He would not have approved of my anger. He preferred forgiveness. I'm not as big-hearted as he was.'

There was a long pause and a strange silence, the sort of silence Michael had witnessed among soldiers, before they launched a full-scale assault. Hillary kept her audience in suspense. Finally she spoke again.

'There is something also about dad that none of you know. Something he wished to keep secret. He was afraid it glorified war. Besides, it was a reminder of a time that still gave him all those sleepless nights.

'He won a medal. Not just any medal. The Victoria Cross.'

There were mutterings from every corner of the church. Hillary had to raise her voice over the noise.

'He had rescued a group of badly injured men at a shelled gunnery post. One by one he carried them to safety, facing fire each time, his uniform soaked in their blood. Were these the actions of a coward?'

The responses were many and clearly audible.

'No, no!'

'Absolutely not'

Hillary continued, obliged to speak loudly over the talking congregation.

'Dad, I stand here, brave because of you. I stand here facing down my grief, just as you faced down your fear for those injured comrades. I honor you as a father, a man of God, and, yes! … As a fighter!'

There was a stunned silence as Hillary stepped down from the lectern. Then something very strange happened, something rarely witnessed in a suburban English church. The sound of clapping started in one corner and it spread quickly, igniting throughout the church. It was a tumultuous applause. Everyone was standing.

Michael noticed a commotion in front of him. Someone was trying to extricate themselves from a serried row. It was causing consternation as people were jostled and had their feet crushed by a large moving body. It was Colonel Traverse, in a great hurry to remove himself from the church.

He looked ungainly, and flustered, his lanky figure making him clumsy in such a tight space. Unfortunately for him, the applause slowly quieted just as he was maneuvering past Mrs Stanthorp's ample figure. He fell over her feet and was launched into her, which caused her to let out a piercing shriek. There was another unusual sound for a funeral. The sound of laughter. Traverse tried to salvage what dignity he could, and stood up straight, pulling sharply on his jacket to square it on his frame. He turned on his heel and left the church, the crisp sound of his heels ringing on the stone.

The congregation rose as one to sing the hymn 'Abide with me.'

As the voices swelled, the words carried Michael deep in thought.

> The darkness deepens; Lord with me abide.
> When other helpers fail and comforts flee,
> Help of the helpless, O abide with me.

He saw the newsreels of a strident Hitler, his flattened palms chopping some specter at his side, the mouth, strangely large in a tight, begrudging face, letting out its staccato yells. He saw the mass of German soldiers with their absurd goose steps pounding the road, beating out all in their path and then he saw Ruth standing solemn and sad clutching a suitcase in one hand and the small hand of Ben on the other. Two helpless figures caught up in the maelstrom.

'The bloody shambles of combat!' he said to himself. He felt uneasy about returning to India, and the funeral had compounded those feelings. It was so easy to forget that the threat of violence was the true purpose of his mission there, when there were so many distractions. The easy camaraderie of his fellow officers. The pleasant days spent in Bakloh, playing tennis and drinking in the mess. He no longer wanted to be seduced into ignoring the reality there which was the fear and carnage of warfare. He could no longer hide from the role he played enforcing colonialism. Is this what Macleod meant when he said that Michael was already with the outsiders? But what did he mean that he was praying for Michael's reconciliation? Michael felt emboldened. He was proud to have been Macleod's friend and wanted to take a personal stand like he did. Michael made a decision to leave the army as early as he could. His return to India would be wrenching but he couldn't get out of it. He wished he didn't have to leave Ruth for so long. The first thing he had to do however, was to break off his engagement with Sarah.

The service was ending. The coffin was borne out. As he looked desperately for a chance to speak to Ruth he saw Sarah approaching him. She had already reached the door and the crowd was pressing in behind her.

'Looking for anyone in particular?' said Sarah. She attended to the fitting of her white gloves. 'Well the service was all right,' she continued, 'but poor dad! I saw Hillary's accusing look. Who could fail to see it? After all dad has tried to do for this community. Talk about disloyalty!'

'On the contrary,' said Michael, unable to conceal the anger in his voice, 'I saw a lot of loyalty today. Sarah, I need to talk to you.'

'Well, dear, I can understand how upset you are. You were a friend of Macleod's.' She did not even give him the respect of his title.

Sarah looked sharply at Michael, before her look softened. 'Yes, Michael, we have a lot to organize before you leave and we only have a few days – but not right now, I'm going home. I'll see you later. I don't think I'll go to the vicarage for the wake.'

Michael waited before leaving the church. He was surprised when he found many of the congregation still outside. Even more strange was the sight of Colonel Traverse. He had become a self-appointed usher, trying to organize everyone.

'If you need help walking to the vicarage, we have some drivers here. Move along now. Just follow the crowd if you're not sure of the direction.'

Suddenly Mrs Stanthorp appeared from a knot of people. She was flushed, as if she had still not recovered from Traverse's unfortunate stumble in the church.

'I think it's wrong of you, Traverse, to get involved now. You of all people. Your behaviour towards him was shameful.'

The colonel flushed with anger. 'What on earth do you mean? I won't be misrepresented like this!'

A middle aged man called out from the group that was assembling opposite the colonel, in confrontation.

'Shameful. That's right'

The reaction gave Mrs Stanthorp encouragement.

'I think I speak for the community when I say that we don't want you grieving with us.'

The crowd voiced its agreement.

'Here! Here!'

The colonel did not recognise the mood of the crowd and the hopelessness of his position. His pompousness increased. 'I've never been afraid of doing my duty,' he said.

Mrs Stanthorp struck a tall, disdainful pose that reminded Michael of an operatic diva. She spat the colonel's words back at him.

'Duty? What you did to the vicar was malice. You owe his family an apology. You owe all of us an apology.'

Again there were murmurings of assent.

Michael felt no sympathy for the colonel, who, for once, was silenced. Traverse was now forced to turn on his heel and retreat, with as much dignity as he could salvage from the unexpected onslaught.

He would not be shamed, though. The colonel knew that Macleod had been vindicated in the eyes of the community, and Michael could already sense his burning anger. Traverse would be unbowed. He would soon be pointing the finger of judgment elsewhere. Michael only hoped that this incident would have removed the poison from his sting.

CHAPTER 20

IT WAS ONLY FOUR DAYS until Michael would have to leave for India. He had not seen Ruth since glimpsing her at the funeral. His aunt's words had been playing on his mind. 'You love her. You can not deny it.' He still hadn't spoken to Sarah and he wondered if she was avoiding him.

He felt a terrible sense of impending loss when he thought of leaving Ruth behind. It was like a grief, waiting to wash over him. Soon he would be watching the sparkling expanse of water growing ever larger as the white cliffs of Dover turned from being a huge majestic wall to a small white streak of paint on the horizon.

He went to the hall telephone, making sure there was no one about to listen to his conversation. He was relieved to hear Ruth's voice on the other end of the telephone.

'Ruth. It's Michael. Listen. I have to talk to you. Alone. Is there any way you can arrange it? This morning? I'll be right over.'

Ruth smiled as she opened the door, and Michael only just resisted an impulse to embrace her. He was shown into the quiet, sunlit sitting room.

'Tea?' Ruth was playing the hostess.

'No, not now, thank you.' Michael felt very nervous.

'I wanted to speak to you in church. It was such a good service,' said Michael.

'Yes,' said Ruth. 'Reverend Macleod had often visited us – just social visits. He was kind, so understanding. He listened to all my worries with great patience. He was tolerant, too. He understood and accepted my situation as a mother on my own, as a Jewish woman. Even more important to me, he understood what brutality can do. So many people don't know. *Keine Ahnung*. No idea, as we say in Germany. It can be a lonely feeling when you can't share such memories.'

Michael felt hurt she could not tell him about the role she had played giving Macleod information about Germany but he reasoned it was her duty to keep quiet about that.

'Yes. I miss him,' said Michael, but he was distracted. At last he launched into the true purpose of his visit. He felt time was pressing him.

'Ruth, I'm going back to India in four days. I wanted to see you before I leave for India. I am going to miss you so much.'

'What do you want, Michael?' said Ruth.

'I want to marry you.'

Ruth looked taken aback. She looked at Michael and answered slowly, 'Michael, this is so difficult for me. I do want to marry you, but how can I commit to you when you are engaged to someone else? How am I supposed to wait in line while you go away for two years and decide if you want to marry Sarah or me? I need security, I have a little boy to look after.'

'But I am calling off the engagement. I want to marry you and look after you and Ben. Just give me a chance to show you! Ruth, we can't throw this away. After Canon Macleod's funeral, I know I want to leave the army and India. I want to go and set up a new life, maybe in America. Let's go together Ruth! Or Africa, I have an uncle who started a tea farm in Kenya and it sounds idyllic. Come with me Ruth, I love you.'

There was a long silence.

'Michael, how could I disguise my feelings for you? Don't you think I've been dreading your return to India? So has Ben. The thought of marrying you makes me so happy. Ben's father was never honorable. What you say sounds wonderful, but it is not realistic. You first have to call off the engagement. You mean a lot to me but you're going off to India for two years. I need someone who will be here near me and care for Ben and I.

'I will Ruth, I am decided, I just have to tell Sarah. I'll come back Ruth, soon. I promise. Wait for me! We'll stay in Camberley if you want. I'll look after Ben and you. Maybe you could come and visit me in India. Or maybe we could marry now and you could come out to India as my wife?'

Ruth looked down, unable to confront Michael directly with what she now wanted to say.

'But how could I be a regimental wife? I don't want to hide anymore. I can't run away. How could I betray my Jewish roots by denying them after all I went through in Germany? I would feel a traitor to my people. The strange thing is that I'm not a traditionalist. It's not the Jewish religion that would stop me marrying you. It would only work if you came back to England as a civilian. And I don't know if I could wait for two years, I would miss you too much. But I know I can not come to India with you.'

'But you just said you loved me! What's the problem with coming out to India? You won't even make that sacrifice. You can't love me.'

It was too late to resign from the army now, he was already committed, and to stay now would be tantamount to desertion. Besides, he had to carry out the promise he made to John Fairbrother. He had to return.

'I do. I do so much. But I would be unhappy. I would make you unhappy.'

'How could you make me unhappy if you were with me? That's impossible. Look, you left Germany.'

'Exactly, Michael. I left Germany. I ran away from my people, my fellow countrymen. I surrendered to their persecution. I don't want to run away again if it means hiding a part of myself. I don't want any lies. I have to have my pride.'

Michael felt angry. He was getting nowhere. 'But Ruth will you wait for me, please say you will?'

Ruth was silent.

Michael's tone changed again, and his voice softened. 'Ruth, please think about what I have said. Give my love to Ben. I'll see my own way out.'

He turned abruptly, unable to look at her again. If he had, he would have seen her standing, looking at him leave with an expression of utter dejection.

The front door closed behind Michael. The warmth of the muted English sunshine, the sound of the pigeons, which usually reminded him of deliciously warm afternoons on the lawn with tea and cakes, brought him no happiness. It was the scene of an epilogue for him now. It would be a long time before he would see Ruth or Ben. He knew that.

CHAPTER 21

MICHAEL WAS COUNTING ON India to distract him from his thoughts of Ruth. He would, at least, be able to fulfill the mission John Fairbrother had given him. He would visit Jane to square everything. He was worried that she and her mother might have been facing unbearable social pressures since their relationship to John had been exposed. They might even have felt obliged to move away and in which case it could be impossible to trace them. He felt a big responsibility towards them, and he would not feel happy until his task was completed. After that, he would make his own plans.

Yet, in spite of this errand and his impatience to face the Pathan once more, he felt like a refugee from his rightful home. He missed Ruth far more than he thought he would and he had written a letter to her that he had posted in Marseilles. He thought about her reaction when she received it. He stood by the deck railing as the ship docked in Bombay, and remembered his words.

'Dear Ruth,' he had said. 'I hope this letter is not an embarrassment to you. I realise awkward questions might be asked. You may even resent it after our last meeting. I only know I have to write it.

'My feelings for you have not changed. In fact, they've been brought more sharply into focus since leaving England. I miss you. I miss Ben. I feel I'm not fulfilling my duty going back to my regiment, that I'm a deserter for leaving you. The world is upside down. In short, I love you.

'Please give me hope that you will wait for me. I will do all I can to make sure we are together again – permanently. How often do we have the chance of happiness? How often do people throw that chance away and live to regret it?

'I wonder if you have had news of your parents. I wish I could be there to comfort you.

'Now for a stupid confession. Is that wretched Gabriel still beating a path to our door? I have sleepless nights thinking about him (well I lose sleep thinking about you too!). If he asks you out, say there's more

Dresden china to evaluate. Say anything! Put him off! Aunt Estelle will back you up. She's a huge fan of yours. I have written to her so that if you want to get in touch with her, she'll be prepared. (Alright! You can see straight through me. I want her to be a sort of chaperone so that she'll keep any rivals at bay!)

'Please write back and reassure me, or I'll be miserable. I'm sorry for my shortcomings. I'm sorry for any seeming lack of love. Just know that you are the only girl I have ever loved, and I want to marry you as soon as we can arrange it. With love. Michael.

'P.S. I have written to Sarah to say that our engagement never really got off the ground, that we were too young and hasty and that it was now over. She must already know in her heart what the truth is. I have not told her about you. First things first. PPS Tell Ben that I will be checking up on his over arm bowling when I return, so he should keep practicing!'

As he stood on the deck and reflected, he was happy that the letter had conveyed his feelings, but he was desperate to have Ruth's reaction.

The ship had docked. There was finality to his severance from England. There was no green in the landscape that confronted him from the deck. There were only browns and the glaring metal of the railway track that ran up the side of the wharf. It mirrored the heat that was already impinging on everyone's senses, even though it was still morning. Everywhere there was commotion – horse drawn carriages rattling up and down the dock, camels lending an exotic air, moving cranes, an old black locomotive, now clattering along the track, dark figures in white robes scurrying to get out of its way.

'Hell of a long way from Tipperary!'

A tall, lank officer from an Indian regiment stood next to Michael. His voice was Irish and it was already slurred by drink. He was a medical officer, like so many of his compatriots.

'You know what I'm seeing out there?' he said. 'A huge broiling Petri dish, churning out every disease and germ known and unknown to man. My God, I've got my work cut out for me!'

He wiped his forehead with a large white handkerchief as if to underscore his dire prediction.

'I can see the enemy already,' he continued. 'Dysentery, malaria, sores, typhoid, sunstroke. Throw in typhus, malaria, rabies and pneumonia, not to mention bubonic plague, and cholera. Ha! And you thought the enemy was up there on the northwest frontier! We're on a fool's errand. Holy Mary, weren't we always on a fool's errand here in India.?'

'What do you mean?' asked Michael, goading him.

'I mean this is 1934, for God's sake,' growled the doctor. His arm clumsily gestured toward the panorama of the quayside, which made him, in his state of inebriation, unsteady on his feet. 'There was a time when all this could be excused,' he said. 'You know! The spread of democracy and civilization, the rule of law. That was the reward. And the price? Greed, oppression, the occasional brutality. Nothing too extraordinary. It seemed a reasonable bargain for all concerned. Am I right?' The doctor glared at Michael, who dared not answer his question. 'And now what? We're too late for any glory. Wrong place, wrong time, old boy.' He said 'old boy' mocking the accent of the British upper class.

He then gave Michael a look of defiance, (or was it sadistic glee?), before turning on his heel and retreating to his cabin. No doubt he would fortify himself with some more Irish whiskey, thought Michael, smiling to himself. Yet the doctor's words had unsettled him, reminding him that this land was alien, dangerous, and that their purpose here was, at best, questionable.

The train was soon crossing the Sind desert, a flat expanse of gray soil, with occasional groves of stunted trees, surviving inexplicably in the intense heat.

The discomfort on the train was only slightly alleviated by the soda water and ice from a tin bucket in the bathroom. As the train strained forward, belching black smoke across the plain, Michael felt the transience of the world he now inhabited. It was a world of suitcases, of brief meetings with strangers, of station platforms with the high-pitched voices of vendors, of chaotic crowds surging to board the train with shoving and shouting. The suffocating heat brought with it the smell of dust, of wood smoke and of dung, which was the signature of India. He was being drawn into the heart of the country, but he felt the pull of home, of Ruth, like the huge gravitational force of a distant planet.

Michael had only to wait, to sit on the cane chairs, or sprawl on his bunk.

The train stopped at a new station, with hissing and clunking. He could hear the usual shouts, and chaos of the platform. But as he looked out of the window, he was startled. He saw something he would have overlooked on his previous tour of duty. A group of white-turbaned Muslims stood in unison. They all faced west, and then crouched on the ground. They were chanting their prayers. Here in the chaos, in the urgency and the jostling of the crowds, these men were abandoning themselves to prayer. They were the same religion as those Pathan fighters he had to subdue on the frontier, the men who mutilated and tortured any hapless Gurkha, who could not be rescued in time. Flaying and beheading were their specialty. And yet they were as rigorous as these co-religionists in observing their worship of a higher authority at each call to prayer. He was disconcerted in feeling an affinity, a respect for the worshippers. This small group of men in prayer, seen from a distance, had brought him a strong sense of God's presence. They had something he didn't have, but wanted and needed. He didn't understand how or why.

'Look at that!' A young soldier spoke out next to Michael. He was due to get out at the next station, but he was already travel-weary. Sweat stained his uniform dark.

'Kneeling on that filthy platform, in one mindless group. They're the same types who riot in mass hysteria, and give us such a hell of a head ache.'

Usually Michael would have smiled affably, but something seemed to be changing in him. 'I don't agree,' said Michael. 'We have the same God. They deserve to be treated with dignity.'

'You haven't had to control the mobs like I have, with all due respect, sir.'

'Respect!' Michael repeated softly to himself.

The bus to Bakloh was painted bright red, with pictures of cows and temples painted lovingly on it. The Indian carpenters had built a rattling, groaning superstructure over an old Chevrolet chassis, and each part seemed to move separately at the grinding of the engine. The tires were alarmingly bald. This was Michael's transport on the steep, winding roads of the mountains, where loose rocks and screed constantly avalanched on to the road in the path of those thin tires. But at least it was there, and ready, which was not always the case in India. He would soon be in the hill station and there was a reason for his impatience to arrive. He wanted to see if a letter from Ruth had arrived.

A young subaltern waited with Michael. 'Oh, my God! We're not getting into this old jalopy. I've seen better transport in the junk yard. This is a joke, sir!'

'Wait till you see the driving! Hope you've got a strong stomach,' said Michael.

Michael was traveling first class – a luxury that meant a thinly padded seat next to the driver. The young subaltern was to sit behind him in second class. He squeezed on to a padded bench with an upright wooden back that had five inches of knee room. Behind him was space for luggage – sacks of rice, and smelly cans of kerosene, on which sat the driver's mate, grinning widely, either at the thought of a thrilling ride or at the anticipated pleasure of seeing the alarm of the white sahibs as the bus hurtled along the precipitous roads.

The driver was a neatly turbaned Sikh, with a carefully trimmed beard – a soigné appearance that would belie his driving style.

They were off. Fifty yards and the bus stopped. A crowd outside surged forward. People piled on as sacks, squawking hens, screaming babies were passed through the windows. The bus rocked alarmingly as some men clung to the outside of the bus. The engine groaned again, and the bus jolted as the gears engaged. They went another fifty yards. This time the driver stepped out and, with an air of self-importance, stepped into a shack that was the bus line's office, to check on paperwork. The tickets then had to be inspected scrupulously, and there were shouts and wild gesticulations as stowaways were thrown off.

By this time there was a goat in the back, bleating in consternation.

The bus passed the shacks. It was filled with the stench and smoke of the impoverished outskirts of the Pathankot. It reached the wider road, lined with mango trees. Women in bright shawls, men leading overloaded donkeys, squatting sight-seers, all watched the progress of the swaying bus. It honked loudly at the tongas, overladen with people and bales of hay. All divisions were now irrelevant, thought Michael. They were all in one bus, one crowded, jostling piece of humanity.

They climbed into the forested foothills that eventually led up to the Himalayas. A gap in the trees revealed a hazy white mass in the background, the highest mountain chain on earth, just a hundred miles away.

As they lurched and swerved round bends, above precipitous drops, Michael thought 'What if I should die now? A Gurkha , dying on a rusting, gaudy old jalopy like this! What an inglorious death that would be!' He rebuked himself. 'As if any death could be glorious!' He tried to be logical. 'I can't die now,' he told himself. 'Too much unfinished business and I have to do something about Ruth.' Again he corrected himself. 'First things first. I have to keep my promise and fulfill the duties I have here. Then I will take the next step. '

A sign on the roadside said 'Drive carefully'. It seemed like a challenge to the driver. He had one hand on the bulb horn outside the window. The other hand was on the gear shift. The steering wheel was, at that moment, unmanned and twisting at each bump in the road. Then the driver put the gear into neutral and turned the engine off to descend a steep slope. He would save petrol alright, thought Michael. He would save petrol and lose the bus and all its passengers!

The young subaltern was looking green. He was groaning. People in the third class, towards the back of the bus, were being sick. The young subaltern could no longer hold out. He staggered forward to the driver. He pleaded with gestures and monosyllables: 'Stop! Stop!'

The brakes were applied and the bus shimmied to a halt, sliding on loose gravel. It finally stopped with a lurch. The young man staggered out and the noise of his stomach emptying was quickly drowned out by giggling in the bus. The laughter grew louder and louder until Michael found himself joining in, as one with the crowd. When the young man boarded once more, with a brief, sheepish smile of relief, there was clapping.

As the bus descended once more, Michael noticed a red bus like theirs laboring up the slope. There was no room, surely, for both vehicles, and, as luck would have it, Michael's bus was on the outside of the road, where a cliff dropped vertiginously below them. The buses approached each other. Their bus squeezed to the dangerous side of the mountain, where it was on loose, slippery gravel. Michael closed his eyes and he could hear a communal gasp of alarm from all the passengers. There was a mutual honk of horns, no crash, no braking. The buses had passed each other, and the driver was smiling broadly, as if he had just played the biggest joke on everyone.

Finally both soldiers were dropped off at a junction where a road led up to Bakloh and the hill station. There was supposed to be a truck waiting for them, but it had not come. The two men left their baggage by the side of the road to walk up a steep footpath. The track was so familiar it almost felt like home. It was exactly how Michael remembered it. It was only he who had changed.

They were close now, passing the football ground, leveled out of the hillside – the only way to make flat ground in that terrain. In amongst one clump of trees was an unexpected sight. There was a cluster of date palms. Legend had it that they were planted by Alexander the Great's men, back in 500 b.c. They had been far from home, from their families, their farms. They had penetrated further than any ancient army. Michael thought of those campaign-weary soldiers, from that distant time. They had almost reached the limit of their endurance, when they had come to this place. Even their great general would not be able to force them past the borders of India. Michael felt their weariness.

There was no pleasure when confronted with familiar sights – the small colorful bazaar, where the shopkeepers on the porches greeted the two men. Michael managed a perfunctory *salaam*. They reached the final crest, with the parade ground, carved out long ago by the engineers, and staggered into the mess.

A young subaltern leapt up from the table when he saw them.

'You're here. Wonderful! What happened to the truck. Where's your baggage?'

Michael smiled broadly, shaking hands and introducing his young companion.

'Tea and fruitcake! Superb!' said Michael. He consoled himself. It could almost be Camberley, he thought.

The subaltern also handed him three letters, and Michael felt a stab of nervousness.

'Thought you'd like to have these before you went back you your bungalow, sir! Amazing, isn't it that we have air mail now? Two years ago we had to wait ages for news from home.'

Michael recognized letters from Sarah and his mother, and a third he guessed was from Ruth. He thought how one of the envelopes in his hand would have been held by Ruth, perhaps days ago. He tore open her letter, ripping the envelope in his impatience.

'Dear Michael. Thank you for your letter, which I received with a mixture of emotions. We've recently celebrated Jewish New Year in our house, and grandmamma made the traditional dishes – a sweet chicken dish with cinnamon and raisins. Sweet food is supposed to symbolize the sweetness of the coming year. I can only hope grandmamma's prayers will help to make it a sweet one. She is religious and has a great deal of faith. She tried so hard to make the celebration happy. She even got hold of some pomegranates from London. She had tried to buy them at the local green grocer, but gave up when the man said 'Granite, Mrs? What's that about granite? Some sor' of table ornament you're after, Mrs?'

'I have to find something to smile about because I keep thinking of you getting further and further away and of my poor family in Germany.

'Ben misses you as well. Gabriel keeps coming to visit us, but Ben does not like him very much. Grandmamma is encouraging him to come and stay and you can guess why. He keeps asking me out and I try to remain as formal as I can. I wish you would return. I think the idea of going to America that we discussed is a very good one. We could both start a new life together and perhaps bring mamma and papa there. It would be such a haven for them. Isn't it funny that Franklin Roosevelt was inaugurated the third day of the third month of '33, just 33 days after Hitler came to power. I think it's an omen.

'I will not comment on your decision to write to Sarah. Just know that I am relieved.

'I miss you. With my love, Ruth'

The letter comforted Michael and made him more determined to advance their plans, but the news of Gabriel irritated him. Michael then turned to the letter from Sarah. He frowned as he read it:

'Dear Michael. Silly Boy! You try to be so noble, but you can not see the wood for the trees. I know you are worried about how I will cope with India, and it is very sweet of you and just shows me your devotion. But you're being over-protective. I will not hear another word about breaking our engagement. That is enough!

'Life in Camberley goes on as usual. Daddy went to a big meeting of Sir Oswald Mosley. He is putting on that shirt more often than when you saw him. Mummy was in hot water with him a few days ago. She said the shirt was perfect for gardening because it did not show the dirt. He said she was being disrespectful. I patched things up and told him how handsome he looked in it. That bucked him up. He needs a bit of cheering up because people in the town have had the nerve to cold-shoulder him since the Macleod funeral. It's a good thing he has friends in the British Union of Fascists. A group of them really look up to him, hanging on his every word. It's really quite funny!

'That neighbour, Ruth, is still here. She will never fit in Camberley. She is seen a lot with a tall dark-haired young man and I was told she was at the pictures with him the other day and someone said they were holding hands, but I could not confirm that and, as you know, I am not one to spread gossip.

'There has been the most awful scandal here. You're missing a lot here, you see, not just me! Apparently that bank manager in town, Bovis, was doing a Noel Coward play and fell for the leading lady – a woman you do not know. It must have been due to all the on stage clinches and ca-noodling. Anyway, they were cuddling on a park bench when the local reporter snapped a picture of them. He published the result on the front page of the local rag with a caption 'Cold snap leads to warm embraces'. We all laughed so much , everyone that is except the jilted spouses.

'And so, my heart, I will end saying that this spouse-to-be will not be jilted. She knows your true feelings. Toodle pip, as they say. Sarah.'

Michael sighed as he put the letter down on the table. He opened his mother's letter which conveyed none of the pessimism she had shown recently. It was a calm, affectionate letter, with assurances of prayers for his well being and hopes for a speedy return.

After his tea, Michael strolled over to the back verandah, where he looked through the glass. He saw the slopes of forest and terraced field dropping away below him, and two miles away, a ridge at his level. It was just as he had described it to Ruth. He wished she was there to see it. He saw a river gushing down a cleft in the foothills. Far to the left he saw the white hazy mountains he had glimpsed from the road. The low sun was golden. It was the same sun that was warming Ruth in the last days of the English summer.

For the first time, Michael felt no sense of home in Bakloh. He was an exile. He was hoping the reunion with his fellow officers would cheer him up, make him feel less isolated. But it had not. He thought of the words of John Fairbrother's mother. What were they doing in this far-flung land? Why was this piece of England grafted so incongruously onto this foreign soil, with its little English church, its bungalows, its sports grounds?

They, the British, would be as ephemeral as those ancient Macedo-nians, leaving, perhaps, a grove of trees here, a terraced field there and, of course, burial grounds. He felt a chilled by the last thought. He was due to go into action soon, and casualties had been very high recently.

CHAPTER 22

Michael had some free time. He had found, to his relief, that John's girl-friend and her mother were living in the house where he had originally met them. He would leave Bakloh and go up the road to Dalhousie, a pleasant hill station, set on five hills with spectacular alpine views. The regiment used Dalhousie for recreation, and Michael had gone there countless times to drink at the bar of a hotel, to go to a dance, to a party, or set off on its mountain paths. Today would be different. It would be arduous and it would have to be discreet.

After telling his servant in unfaltering Hindi to bring him some tea, Michael went to his bedroom to retrieve a small leather suitcase from under his bed. He unlocked it and carefully transferred some of its contents into a briefcase He then glanced in a mirror on the wall to make sure his appearance was neat. He was in uniform and that was important, to dress for the part he had to play. He noticed he was already tanned from the parade ground drills and a white strip marked the position of the chin strap on his hat. It reminded him how long he had already spent away from England. He sighed.

The servant brought in the tea on a tray, and Michael helped himself to a generous amount of evaporated milk and sugar, to fortify himself. He felt like having whiskey, but it would not be right to arrive in Dalhousie smelling of alcohol.

The sergeant was at the wheel of the truck.

'All right, sir?'

Michael clambered up beside him. Soon they were bumping over the narrow road that threaded itself around the hillsides. The forested hills were green and lush after the monsoon rains. Michael wished he were hiking up a path with nothing but the high-pitched birdsong and caw-ing of the crows to interrupt the silence.

'Going for a spot of r and r, sir?' asked the sergeant.

'Just a visit' said Michael. He was unusually silent and listened to the soldier describe in detail, his struggles with a bout of malaria. He replied just enough to indicate that he was listening, but his mind wandered as he rehearsed in his mind the words he would soon have to use.

In Dalhousie, Michael walked straight towards his destination. He passed a church, faced in stone, with gothic-style windows. It would not have looked out of place in an English village. Nor would the head-stones. Their silent testimony to the dead somehow disturbed him.

He was soon descending a steep, narrow road, a rocky slope on his left and chalet-style houses set on the steep hillside on his right. He came to one house behind a crenellated white stone wall. It was small, but elegant, with stone facing below a wooden superstructure. It had a sharply pitched roof and three gables. The sign on the gate said 'The Pines' and it opened with a creak. As he prepared to walk down the steps to the front door, his mind went back to the time he had been at the Fairbrother's door with Macleod. It was natural to think about that now. He only wished Ruth was around the corner, as she had been then. He would promise her anything, he would never leave her again. He gripped his briefcase more tightly as he reminded himself of his present duty.

The door opened quickly after two knocks. It was clear that he was expected. A white-turbaned servant stood back to usher Michael in, and a woman was waiting in the dark-paneled hallway. She appeared to be in her fifties and she was dressed like an English lady, wearing a pale blue sweater with pearls, over a beige tailored skirt. Yet she was brown-skinned and her dark eyes were piercing. Her black hair was streaked with gray and scraped back into a chignon. As Michael approached her, he realized she had sprinkled herself liberally with lavender water. He was reminded of the old ladies in church, back home in Camberley. They, too, used lavender water. It mingled oddly with the aroma of wood smoke, that permeated the house, as it did everywhere in India. The woman held out her hand, limply.

'Michael, how awfully good to see you again. What do we say? 'Hail, fellow, well-met!' It's been so jolly difficult lately. Well, you know, don't you?'

Her idiomatic English, with its clipped accent, would have amused Michael, on other occasions. It was as if she were trying too hard to be English, yet in doing so, she betrayed her Anglo-Indian origins.

The woman was Mary Parry.

Michael was shown into a modest-sized drawing room that could have been in an English cottage. The slip covers were made of quality floral chintz and an embroidered fire-screen was in front of the carved wooden fireplace. A gleaming copper fire set and scuttle were placed beside the hearth, testaments to the diligent polishing of a servant. But the real focus of the room was the large window overlooking the valley. There was a verandah with wicker chairs just in front of the window, but otherwise the view was unimpeded. The valley was far below out of sight and a steep hillside, green with pines and oak, rose up opposite. Beyond, in the distance, stood the snow-capped peaks of the Himalayan range.

'It's lovely, isn't it? said Mary. 'A room with a view! I sit out there every morning to have breakfast, and my troubles melt away. We've had such a time of it. Well, of course, you know!'

He suddenly feared Jane would not join them. Her mother had an over-protective look in her eye and, in spite of her benign manner, looked at him with distrust. If Jane did not appear, he would have to re-arrange a meeting, and insist on her presence.

Mary's voice broke Michael's thoughts.

'I was glad to get your telephone call, Michael.'

Before Michael could answer, a figure appeared noiselessly in the doorway. It was Jane. She stood before him in a simple white blouse and brown, close-fitting skirt with kick pleats that showed off her figure. She looked as beautiful as he remembered her. She seemed more rounded than before, more womanly. She held out her hands, and started to mouth a greeting, but as she did so, her eyes welled with tears.

'Excuse me!' she stuttered. 'It's the uniform. It reminds me...'

'I know,' said Michael. 'Please, Jane. Sit down. I have something to tell you.'

'I, too, have something to tell you,' said Jane, quietly. Her mother looked at her sharply.

'I'll order the tea,' said Mary. 'Tea and sympathy.'

Michael looked at Jane to see if her mother's choice of words embarrassed her, but Jane was absorbed in her own thoughts. Meanwhile Mary was busying herself, reminding Michael of his own mother's way of dealing with awkwardness. Mary called out in Urdu and the same turbaned man who had come to the door appeared. He left only to return with a rattling trolley of tea cups, sandwiches and cakes.

Jane was still sitting, deep in thought. Michael began to speak to her softly, as if he were waking somebody deep in sleep.

'Jane, I have something for you. I don't know if you know this, but John had made plans for you. He seemed to know something would happen to him.' Michael was briefly reminded of the foreboding he had about his own death, and he quickly suppressed the thought.

Jane's voice was flat.

'All I wanted was him. Nothing else matters.'

Michael looked at Mary, and she nodded her encouragement for him to continue.

'It's a package. I have it here.'

He unbuckled the briefcase and took out a fat manila envelope. He held it out to her.

She did not take it. She was suspicious.

'What is it?'

'Take it! Please.'

Mary interrupted. 'Let me take it. Michael. Jane would want me to.' Jane made no opposition, and Mary took the package, walking briskly to a desk, seizing a letter opener and ripping the paper noisily. It was a large wad of money, and valuable bonds.

'It is as it should be,' she said. She then started to look through the bundle more closely, quickly calculating its value.

Michael then pulled another package out, wrapped in brown paper, with string. 'I have something else, Jane. It's his diary. There's a letter to go with it.'

This time Jane held out her hand. She clutched the parcel to her chest.

Mary was incurious about the second package. She locked the money in her desk and spoke to Michael. 'Michael, the fruit cake was made in your honor. Oh, golly! You haven't even had your tea. Let me be mother and pour for you.'

Michael looked anxiously at Jane. It was obvious that her mother would not leave them alone so he would have to say everything in front of her. 'I have a message that John wanted me to give you. He wanted to marry you. You know that. But he said that if he were to die, he would want you to do something.'

Jane looked at Michael intently. Her dark eyes immobilized him, willing him to speak,

'He wanted to make sure that you were free. He did not want to involve you with his family in England. All the trouble that would cause. Not that they're bad people.

'I understand,' said Jane.

Mary spoke up with vigor.

'Yes. He was right. I knew he was a practical man. Better let sleeping dogs lie.'

'I was to give you their address and act as an intermediary if you wished.' He pulled a neatly folded piece of paper from the pocket of his khaki shirt and offered it to Jane.

'No, no!' said Mary. 'That won't be necessary.'

'Free' said Jane, as if speaking to herself. Then she laughed. Michael looked at her in surprise.

'Free? No! I'll never be free. And thank God for it.'

'I know,' said Michael. 'The loss is always with you.'

'No!' said Jane. 'You've missed the point.'

Mary suddenly looked alarmed. 'No, Jane! Don't. I've warned you!'

'Mummy, I have to.' Jane rose to her feet and started to leave the room, but her mother quickly stood in her way.

'I've told you, Jane. This is foolishness. I won't have it.' Jane just edged around her mother, and left the room.

Mary looked unusually agitated. 'She's not well. Not herself. Gone completely doolally. What is a mother to do? O, I don't mean that either.'

Michael was totally perplexed. He had heard from Estelle that women of a certain age could have funny turns, but Mary seemed to be another person. Nervous. Fretful.

'This is so awkward, Michael. I want to be sure of your absolute silence in this matter. Silent as the grave. Oh, dear. I shouldn't have said that under the circumstances! But Michael, I have no control over Jane. She is being stubborn like a mule. I need to protect her. I can't tell you the trouble I've taken.'

The door opened once more. Jane came in, smiling and she was followed by an elderly woman in a sari, with brown, wrinkled skin. She was holding something in her bony arms. Michael quickly saw it was a sleeping baby.

'This is our son, Michael. John's son,' said Jane.

Michael could not speak.

She sat down on the sofa next to Michael and the old woman handed her the child. The sad. defeated expression on her face had gone. She smiled down at her child and brushed the plump cheek with her finger. She then looked up at Michael and laughed.

'Here,' she said. 'Hold him.'

There was a fumbling as Michael clumsily took hold of the baby. Jane positioned his arms.

He stared at the child. His eyelids fluttered open briefly and with a little squeak, as puppies make, he settled back to sleep. His tiny fingers twitched on the blanket. Gently Michael touched his soft downy hair with his free arm. This baby was the link between life and death. His birth was the one sure fruit of Empire. He was the co-mingling. The hope. The Muslim tribesmen who killed John would have summed it up. *Inshallah,* as God wills it.

'He's beautiful. What's his name?'

'David', said Jane.

He glanced up, and Mary was looking uncomfortable.

'He's my niece's child, you understand, Michael? My niece in Delhi who has health problems. Her family already has their hands full, so we're looking after the child.'

'I understand,' said Michael.

Mary scolded her daughter. 'Really, Jane. This is so jolly foolish.' Mary looked stern. 'Above all we don't want John's family to know. We don't want them interfering. It could create all sorts of difficulties.'

Michael did not placate her. He looked down at the baby.

'I have never been so excited about an introduction, have I, David?'

Jane suddenly gasped.

'O, Michael, I'm so sorry.'

At the moment she, spoke, Michael understood. He felt a warm sensation on his lap, and looked under the bundled baby to see a stain spreading across his khaki trousers. He laughed and Jane laughed too, while her mother snatched a tea towel from the trolley to fuss over him.

'Don't worry, Mary', said Michael, handing the child to her grandmother. 'It might have dampened my uniform, but not my spirits.'

Michael thoughts wandered to the elderly Fairbrother parents, huddled in grief in their genteel English home, their lives shattered by a sniper's bullet in the arid Afghan hills. He felt the baby squirm in his lap, their grand child. He felt his warmth, and the warmth was John's. Here was John's legacy, his destiny. His spilt blood would leave no mark. It had sunk into the greedy dust. It was blown to oblivion. Would he resolve to tell the grandparents? It was his choice. Should he break the trust of these two women, facing their own fears alone, balancing precariously between two cultures?

He continued to look down at the baby. He remembered the story of the two women in the bible, fighting to take possession of a baby, and Solomon testing their love. The true mother put the welfare of the child above her intense need to nurture it. She refused to physically wrest it free, fearing to harm the infant. It was the child's well being that mattered. A child did not need principles. It was too innocent to be caught up in a battle of prejudices. The English, perhaps the Fairbrothers, might think that immersion in the British way, even removal from

India, was the biggest advantage that could be given to a child. But to Michael it was freedom. The ability to freely give and accept the love that came to you. Nothing should threaten the bond between parent and child. Still, he felt a nagging sense of doubt when he pictured the Fairbrother parents, gaunt and riven with grief. He wondered if little David would ever meet his grandparents. He knew how this little baby could change their lives. Later when he rose to leave, as he was being ushered out, Michael slipped the Fairbrothers' address into Jane's hand.

As he walked away his thoughts strayed to the future. He was due to go on maneuvers in the Northwest Province , on the borders of Afghanistan. Conflict was inevitable. His sense of foreboding loomed in front of him, like the hillside opposite the window that dwarfed the house. His future was already set, unmovable.

CHAPTER 23

The evening was balmy and calm as Michael sat on the verandah of his bungalow reading an old copy of *The Times*. He felt slightly tipsy because he had just been to the Gurkha officers' club where he had been entertained by Jemadar Sing, an officer who had attained the highest rank of a Gurkha, with the title, Subadar-major. Michael was surprised by his choice of casual dress. Sing wore a bright red and yellow shirt with mauve plus fours. It made Michael laugh out loud and he told his friend he barely recognized him. Sing had laughed back. 'Gurkha fashion.' he said. 'You should try it Major Rogers. It drives the women wild.'

His dress seemed to augur a raucous night, but instead it had been calm and convivial. Sing had been Michael's second-in-command on a previous campaign in the NorthWest Frontier Province, and a bond had developed between the two men. The bearers had brought orange scented rum, a specialty of the club, and for the first time since he had come to India, Michael felt relaxed. Yet, in the back of his mind. he knew such a feeling would prove fleeting.

As he sat back and enjoyed the memories of the evening, his thoughts were disturbed by his bearer, bringing him a letter on a silver salver. Michael quickly recognized Ruth's writing and perfunctorily dismissed the servant in Hindi. He opened it with trepidation, sensing the news was not good.

'Dear Michael. This is a painful letter to write. I have decided to marry Gabriel. We got engaged yesterday and plan to marry in the spring. I will not go into my feelings. It would not be proper and you can guess them anyway, as although we have know each other for a short time. we understand each other very well.

'I look at Ben and I feel I have a huge responsibility for him, especially with the turmoil my family is in, and the worry about my parents and relations in Germany. Gabriel can offer him the security he needs. I have a duty to do that for him. I will not make this any longer than I have to. Take care, my darling, and God bless you. Ruth.'

Michael put the letter down and looked at the floor, his head resting on his hand. He just wanted to think, but his mind would not focus. It was if he were at a junction between despair and defiance. Just as he was about to give in to his sadness, something in him, perhaps the soldier, made him stand up and resolve to take action. He would not let Ruth succumb to her feeling of insecurity. He would not let her turn her back on their love. He immediately went to write his reply, which he would airmail back to her. He sat at the mahogany desk in his sitting room, which was a stark contrast to the sitting rooms of Camberley. A ceiling fan beat the air above him, and animal skins adorned the white walls, yet his mind wandered easily to England and the personal crisis unfurling so far away.

'Dear Ruth. For once I am going to take your advice and be outspoken. There are too many times I have remained silent. You speak of duty, but it is our duty to follow what we know to be right. Our love is like a truth and we can not escape it. We will show everyone what it means to face down the opposition, the nay-sayers. We will show them all, the racial bigots, the intolerant, the snobbish, what it is to love. Some people have happiness taken away from them and that is tragic. But to throw it away is destructive. Ruth, wait for me! I can be in England next summer. I will do whatever it takes to marry you.

'Sometimes I think we are stupid. The world is going mad now. There are all sorts of horrors in it that you and I have witnessed. In the middle of it all we have our love. Are we going to be like spoilt children, dazzled by everything around us, and treat it as a passing toy? What are we struggling for, you in your flight from the Nazis, and me in this foreign land, if it is not the right to love freely? We are all fools, but we can be wise in one way. Not to compromise. I will be with you soon. Wait for me. Please. With all my love Michael.'

He would do anything to prevent Ruth from marrying Gabriel. If only he could get through the next campaign. He was due to leave in the next few days for the Northwest Frontier, and he could not shake off a sense of foreboding, an uncanny feeling that something was going to happen to him. Superstition can be dangerous for a soldier. It can sap morale and lead to defeatism. It can deaden reactions in the height of combat. The consequences can be fatal.

There used to be comfort in belonging to such an elite regiment. Generations of men had made it into an almost living entity. The men got drunk, played, killed, fought together, as one. There was no room to question an individual's role. That was self-indulgent. Even thoughts of the Almighty were eclipsed by the need to 'get on with the job', to follow the flag.

Yet something had changed in Michael. He could not stop the questions of what he was doing in this far-flung land, and for whom. He kept seeing the corpse of John Fairbrother, the hand reaching over the dust as if to grab a vestige of life. He could not sleep at night. Thoughts kept going around and around in his mind. He began to think he was depressed, that he was suffering from Canon Macleod's malady; from a form of shell shock. He feared he would do something rash; desert, run away, or have some sort of a mental breakdown. He felt it coming. He was in crisis.

It was difficult to confide in a fellow officer, because personal feelings were meant to be reined in, if not stifled completely. But he felt isolated and he had to talk to someone, however ill-advised it might be. He remembered Macleod's words. 'Don't be afraid to be an island, Michael.' What sort of damn-fool advice was that? He had to re-connect with his peers; allow the team spirit to take charge of him once more. He had to put an end to this infernal nagging, inner voice that was driving him mad. So Michael did speak to a fellow officer, obliquely and, he thought, tactfully, admitting to doubts about the British role in India. Tim Nicholl, also a young major, was his confidant, but his reaction was violent, underlining the taboo of looking too hard at any moral issue. 'Action, not words' was the soldier's motto, and too much delving into moral issues, too much philosophizing was seen as feeble-minded. Worse than that, it was seen as effeminate and pretentious. It was as bad as reading poetry and it had a name among the junior officers: 'poodle faking'.

Tim had become angry when Michael voiced his misgivings. Michael only realized later that he had touched a raw nerve when he spoke about his doubts.

'Sometimes I think we've got it all wrong' said Michael. 'Think of the Charge of the Light Brigade. We Brits use that fiasco to glorify war, but it does just the opposite. Six hundred cavalrymen riding into Russian guns because of a mistaken order. Riding in full regalia as if it were some bloody costume party. How pretty do you think they looked after the cannons struck them head on? Remember Kipling's words? "If any ask us why we died, / Tell them 'because our fathers lied'."'

It was only when Tim's voice exploded back at him that Michael knew he had gone too far.

'What the hell are you talking about, Rogers?' he said. 'If you don't know why you're here and what a privilege it is to be with this regiment, you'd better resign your commission now. You're a bloody fool to talk like that. I wish you'd just shut up!'

Michael looked down, deeply embarrassed, as he mumbled an apology. Tim tried to soften the effect of his angry words. 'You're just out of sorts after your leave in England. It happens to all of us.'

Tim must have had his own dark moments. His fair hair and fresh, youthful complexion exuded energy and optimism, but he had seen his share of horrors – comrades killed, brutal ambushes, lining up a man in his gun sights and watching him crumple at the pull of the trigger. He simply refused to dwell on such thoughts. He allowed himself to be caught up in following the group without any soul-searching. Discipline, orders, patriotism, selflessness, they were the ideals of the army, and if Tim did examine them, he would have seen them as essential and as noble.

The mission that Michael and Tim were given was very dangerous. They were on Road Protection duty. Roads had to be secured from rebel tribesmen, who were out to kill as many British soldiers as they could. They would march along the routes in battle formation, and all potential ambush sites had to be searched. Groups of about twelve men, known as piquet's, were left behind at vantage points to ensure continued security. The same road had to be cleared three times a week, and the hidden eyes of the Pathan were watching for any weakness, any slip up. Go over the same ground in the same way twice, and the enemy would be waiting for you.

The terrain looked particularly bleak and arid, as two piquets, one headed by Michael, the other by Tim Nicholl, made their way to a point that had been used before for sabotaging troops.

Tim pointed to a small valley in the distance.

'Know what that is?' he asked Michael.

Michael shook his head. It looked totally insignificant. Perhaps it was the site of some massacre.

'Its part of the ancient Silk Road. You know, the trade caravans, linking the people of the east and west long before we European explorers claimed we discovered the east. It wasn't just goods being exchanged there. Ideas, religious beliefs crossed over, blood co-mingled. How do you think you get all those blue-eyed tribesmen? East meets West. Now that's a joke, isn't it? We know better don't we? Like trying to mix oil and water. Oil and bloody water!'

In spite of the difficulty of the terrain, and the threat of danger, Michael looked at the rocky valley trail and felt there was a certain romance about it. He had a superstitious feeling about places. History seemed to seep into the landscape, casting its long shadow over future events. He had a strong sense that the day's experiences were going to be momentous.

The morning sun, still low on the horizon, was already hot. The distinctive Gurkha hats, with the brim folded at one side, failed to protect them from the glare. Yet eyes were needed now to scan the terrain near and far for any movement, any unusual shadow. The shirts of every soldier had the dark stain of sweat.

It was now time for Michael to lead a group of twenty men to form a piquet on a high ridge beside the road. They had already been there two days before. Michael would lead one group up the higher ridge, and Tim Nicholl would take the other group to the top of a smaller ridge beside it.

The only noise was of the hobnailed boots on stone and fall of loosened screed as the men climbed the two slopes. The group on the lower slope peeled away, and Michael realised with a jab of anxiety that they would be out of sight for a few minutes as they descended into a small hollow before reappearing on the hillside.

Suddenly gunfire rent the silence. It came from the direction of the hollow. Michael and his men dived to the ground, their rifles pointing in the direction of the firing. They crawled or crouched forward up the slope to get into a position over the hollow.

When Michael crested a ridge, the sight was sickening. Every man who had scrambled towards the second hillside had fallen into the trap. Tim Nicholl was lying on his back. Not content to shoot him, the tribesmen had found time to slit his throat, and the unmistakable sight of dark, life blood, soaked the pale, ochre earth beside him. His comrades lay near him in the contorted positions of sudden, brutal death. There was no sign of the killers.

Michael was breathing fast. He looked beyond the scene of the massacre. Nothing. Just an eerie emptiness. He ran further up the hill. He was driven beyond professional duty. He wanted vengeance. The words he had spoken to Macleod came back to him. 'I want to bury as many of those bastards as I can.' He came to a large rock face that he had to skirt around to advance, and as he did he thought he noticed a slight movement. Something flashed in his peripheral field of vision. Fleetingly. It could have been a reflection. He pressed himself against the rock face to remain hidden. Then he saw it clearly. The flash of white was a turban with a piece of cloth hanging at one side. A tribesman. He could not see his face.

The man was scurrying away in supernatural silence. His thin brown legs had the agility of a mountain gazelle, as they picked their way over the rough ground. His rifle, that had so recently killed, was slung casually over a shoulder.

Michael took aim. He had never before had such a deliberate, solitary target. He felt gleeful and exhilarated. His hatred of the enemy urged him on, like a drum, with the beat of his heart. It was battering his chest wall. He squeezed the trigger and felt the sharp kick back of the rifle. There was an echo from the rocks and the acrid smell of gun smoke. The figure fell. It looked little more than a pile of rags. Then there was silence.

Michael took his field glasses. The landscape was truly empty now, he thought. His soldiers were still behind him. He felt an unnerving sense of exhilaration. How terrible was the discovery that killing could be thrilling. He became more excited by something he saw by the crumpled body. It was leather. It looked like a binocular case. The brown, polished surface gleamed in the sun. It looked good.

Michael made a quick calculation. He would be able to run down the steep slope and grab the case in a matter of minutes. His men would have secured the hill by then, and there was little danger of any tribesmen staying behind. In his excitement, he felt he could risk it.

His feet slid as he approached the body. He felt a pang of uneasiness. The eyes of the man were still open – gray green eyes, looking at him. He closed the lids. This man would have spared him no brutality, no pain, no desecration before or after death. He wanted his hatred to come back to him, as blind and unforgiving as the dead man's pale eyes. There was no room for emotion in this arid, unforgiving land. Somewhere, though, words sidled into his mind, irrepressible.

'I am the enemy you killed, my friend.'

The hands of the tribesman were rough, and covered in white dust. They were like the hands of a peasant, and yet the fingers were long and elegant. Piano player's hands, thought Michael, stupidly. His hatred was eluding him and he grabbed the strap of the binocular case, as if he were clawing back his fury. In one quick movement he tore it from the shoulder. The leather felt soft and warm, the buckle glinted in the sun. He turned quickly with his booty and headed to the shelter of a nearby rock. His men would have regrouped at any moment and he had just enough time to examine his booty.

Still breathing heavily, the fingers that had so recently squeezed the trigger opened the buckle. He was puzzled. Inside the case was green silk – luminous, diaphanous silk, of a high quality. It was not what you would expect to find on a tribesman. His fingers probed the cloth impatiently, and he felt something inside, but they were not field glasses. He roughly pulled out the contents, and unraveled the silk, like a child unwrapping a gift swathed in too much paper. His hands were moist and trembling with anticipation or agitation. This would surely be a treasure. He felt the thrill of something like greed.

The roll of silk finally revealed its contents. His prize was in his hands. He froze.

He was holding a small, leather-bound volume. Etched in gilt, all over the cover, were the flowing letters of the Arabic script. He gently opened the volume at random and thumbed through the pages. Letters were illuminated in glowing, peacock colors. He knew now. This was the Koran. It was so precious to its owner that it was to be revered and only touched through the finest silk. It was part of the dead man's soul. His amulet Koran.

And now it was in Michael's possession. It was destined to be his, like a message that had long since borne his name. The enemy lying in the dust had brought him this talisman, the same man who would have labeled him an infidel, worthy only of a horrible death. He would have viewed any tolerance of Michael as an aberration. But he, this lifeless, unknown tribesman, was only the messenger.

Michael suddenly felt sick to his stomach. He wanted to run and keep running. He had no right to be in this land, no right to kill one of its sons. He was the tribesman, the primitive, following blindly the diktats of the politicians, of the businessmen, of his peers. The words of Macleod came to him. 'Thou shalt not kill. Four small words. Pretty uncompromising, aren't they?' His eyes felt hot with tears. He tilted his head back and shut his eyes in an attempt to quell his emotion. The sorrow had taken a long time to come through. Nothing would be the same now.

But Macleod's words brought with them a glimmer of hope. He clutched the small volume, feeling its life-like warmth. He saw now what Macleod meant about reconciliation. The emptiness of the parched mountain slopes echoed the voice in his mind. 'Alone, you know what to do.' The layers of propaganda unraveled. He would be his own master from now on. And he knew what to do.

Michael turned his back on the dead man and headed towards his men. His relief made him reckless as he strode out in the open, oblivious to the risk of further ambush. There was no triumphalism now, but neither was there defeat. The road home was so short he could see two distant figures waiting for him. One of them was propped on legs as thin and spindly as a wading bird's.

The crack of gunfire took Michael by surprise. There was no way to escape the bullets.

Nairobi 1965

THE TORRENTIAL RAIN of a tropical thunderstorm looked like an underwater scene through the car's windshield. David Fairbrother, a young English tourist, listened to the rippling cracks of thunder, wishing that his car had a lightning conductor. He was on his way to visit an old family friend, Michael Rogers, who had known his father. They had served in the army together, before his father, John, had been killed. David had always wanted to visit Michael. He had been brought up by his grandparents and his aunt in Camberley. His aunt had frequently spoken to him about Michael and his time with his father in the Gurkhas in India. He had many questions about his parents he hoped Michael would answer.

David's mother had written to the Fairbrothers after John's death and they had travelled over to India to meet her. They had convinced her to come over to England for a six-month visit, but she was unused to the English climate and contracted pneumonia and died a few months after she arrived there.

David had called from his hotel to finalise arrangements to meet Michael, and he had received some complicated directions, that involved finding a narrow dirt road off the main road. The voice on the other end of the phone had surprised him. It had a distinct 'colonial' twang to it. 'Great to hear your voice, David. Just keep your wits about you if it rains. The murram roads rapidly deteriorate into rivers of mud. Easy to get stuck.'

David was thrilled to be in Kenya. The downpour had stopped as suddenly as it had started, giving way to a hot steamy day. The intoxicating scent of frangipani and the distinctive 'hoop-hoop' calls of the African Hoopoe and a chorus of other birds, filled the air. He began to understand why Michael had moved here many years ago. His aunt had told him that after coming out of the army, Michael had been unable to settle back in England. His close brush with death seemed to have affected him deeply. He had become more outspoken against British rule in India, he had resigned his commission and, worst of all in the eyes of many, he had married in haste and without reflection. He found the life in Camberley too staid and it was too constraining to be so close to his family once he was married. His stint in India made him long for the excitement of lands overseas but he could not face returning to India. That's when he decided to move to Kenya and run a coffee farm.

David had his father's height and chiseled profile but he had striking oval brown eyes that were unmistakably his mother's. In spite of being in the tropical heat, he wore a conservative, short-sleeved shirt and gray trousers. His uneven haircut, with awkward fringe sweeping across his forehead, and large horn-rimmed glasses hid most of his face. Yet he was a fine looking man. His sideburns were the only concession to fashion.

David saw the arching purple bougainvillea that he had been told to look out for. Through the arch he was able to see into a large garden with mango trees, avocado trees and palm trees with flowerbeds full of bright red and yellow canna lillies. He drove up to the colonial bunga-low which had a verandah covered with mosquito netting running the whole length of the house.

Before David could climb out of the car, Michael appeared at the doorway. He was shorter than David had imagined and was dressed very casually with khaki shorts, a t-shirt and bare feet. He invited David into a large sitting room furnished like a Raj style bungalow – the slatted, dark wooden armchairs with loose cushions, the ornately-carved Indian chest, covered with photograph frames. On the walls hung the kukris – the special curved knives that were the Gurkha emblems. Kenyan carvings of elephant and giraffe and native heads were interspersed with the Indian ornaments. What mostly caught David's attention however was the wide assortment of childrens' toys scattered over the floor. Pho-tographs of African babies and children of various ages were on every available space and a sudden sharp cry, clearly of non-avian origin made him start.

Michael smiled 'You probably didn't expect this,' he said, gesturing to the articles on the floor. The coffee farm had not worked out. Neither of them took to farming, and the Mau-Mau insurrection broke out a year after they bought the farm, and a nearby farmer and his wife were hacked to death by a gang of men wielding pangas, machete-like knives. Since he left the Gurkhas, Michael had become aware of a growing feeling of emptiness in side him. He had twinges of the same feeling when he saw ragged orphans standing sadly in London doorways. The feeling had been much stronger when he saw the same children sleeping under pieces of cardboard in Nairobi's backstreets. He knew his emptiness could only be filled by looking after these children. There was his craving faith, his inner Koran swathed in silk, and he had to be true to it. Fate showed the way, as just at that time, a letter arrived from London announcing a new venture of Barnardo's childrens' homes, a home for street children in Nairobi. Was he at all interested to help get it going? The decision was made as he and his wife read the letter. They moved to Nairobi and life had been blissful for them both from then on.

'Now where's the wife? She's been looking forward to seeing you. She's been in the kitchen all morning. She wanted to cook you a special dish of welcome. Family recipe. Some sort of sweet-tasting casserole of chicken with cinnamon and raisins. To celebrate the sweet things in life, she says.'

Michael disappeared through a door and David stood up to look at the pictures on the shelves. There were photographs of Michael's sons, both as boys and adults. The dark haired boy must have been Michael's adoptive son, he thought. There was a pictures of a baby, probably a grand child. His family photos were interspersed with photos of his 'other' family. Smiling black faces of all ages from babies to teenagers, some taken in this house. One end of the sitting room was dominated by a big stone fireplace and on its mantel was a beautiful silver menorah. Set into the stone were little alcoves. Then Michael spotted something on one shelf that he could not make out. It looked like a leather case, a binocular case, with some green silk spilling out. A curious object to display, he thought.

A woman's footsteps rang out on the stone- tiled floor and David turned to see an elegant woman, carrying a smiling two-year-old black baby on her hip. Her dark eyes smiled in welcome. Her hair was gray, but it still had dark streaks, and it was swept up into an elegant chignon. Her features were fine, and firm.

'David, this is Ruth' said Michael.

TIGER OF THE STRIPE

Typeset in the
United Kingdom by
Tiger of the Stripe
in LTC Garamond

www.ingramcontent.com/pod-product-compliance
Lightning Source LLC
Chambersburg PA
CBHW020951180626
46814CB00003B/1045